Tower

STORIES

MERCER UNIVERSITY PRESS

Endowed by

TOM WATSON BROWN

and

THE WATSON-BROWN FOUNDATION, INC.

Tower

STORIES

Andy Plattner

MERCER UNIVERSITY PRESS
Macon, Georgia

MUP/ P637

Published by Mercer University Press
1501 Mercer University Drive
Macon, Georgia 31207

25 24 23 22 21 5 4 3 2 1

Books published by Mercer University Press are printed on acid-free paper that meets the requirements of the American National Standard for Information Sciences—Permanence of Paper for Printed Library Materials.

Printed and bound in the United States.

This book is set in Adobe Garamond Pro.

Cover/jacket design by Burt&Burt.

Print ISBN 978-0-88146-828-1
eBook ISBN 978-0-88146-829-8
Cataloging-in-Publication Data is available from the Library of Congress

For W. S. May

Contents

Acknowledgments

"Hialeah," *Sewanee Review*

"Landslide" and "Fortune," *The Southern Review*

"PSH," *Atticus Review*

"Room," "Selection," "At the Democrat Museum in Madisonville, Kentucky," *New World Writing*

"Secret," *Saw Palm*

"Wake," *apt*

Tower

STORIES

Landslide

In mid-winter of 1972, my unemployed father brought home a Parker Bros. board game called *Landslide.* In the game, players competed for electoral votes and the winner became the president. He probably borrowed it from somebody at the union hall, where he spent a lot of his time. He'd been laid off from his job as a quality control inspector at Goodyear; it was work he said he hated, but after a while it was obvious he'd give anything to have it back. The game looked lame, it wasn't new. The board was warped, and we discovered the player pieces were missing. There was just a single dice to roll and little stacks of cards that said *Politics* and *Win Votes.* I want you all to learn something here, he told us. My father correctly surmised that my sister and I wouldn't care about playing, so he announced that the winner of the game would be president of our house for a week. The president would have no chores, could choose what we had for dinner and what we watched on TV afterwards.

My father, whose name was Douglas Schadler, started going through the magazines and newspapers he kept in stacks in our living room. He found a *Time* article with photos of all the major Democratic candidates. His idea was that everyone could pick who they wanted; we'd cut out the photos and use those as the player pieces. My mother worked ten hours a day at a walk-in clinic in downtown Akron and usually still wore her name-clip (*Alanna, Receptionist*) when we sat down to dinner at night. She wanted to be Ted Kennedy. My father said, You know he's out of the running, sweetheart. I know, she said, looking over the photos. She pointed to Shirley Chisholm, a Black woman in eyeglasses. My sister, a year older than me, jumped in and said she could be for New York City mayor John Lindsay. In Lindsay's photo, he looked actor-handsome. My sister was twelve. My father said to me, All right, Randy, you pick. I pointed at a photo of Governor George Wallace. My mother said, What about Edmund Muskie? To me, Muskie looked like a dentist. In his photo, Wallace was making a speech; his hair was all greased back and he looked super pissed off. No, I said. No way. That's my guy.

You wanted them to be interested, my mother said in the direction of my father. Come on, it's all right, she added in that gentle, clinic-voice of hers. You be Muskie, she said to him. He considered the candidates. Hubert Humphrey, he said. That's probably the closest thing we've got to beating Nixon.

When it was my sister's turn to roll the dice, one of my parents would say, All right, Mayor Lindsay, you're up. It was great to pretend like that: my mother became a senator and my father had once been a vice president. Governor sounded good to me, I liked it. I was certain Alabama was a good place, even if I'd never been there. I got lucky dice rolls and the game seemed easy. I piled up *Win Votes*, used *Politics* at the right times. In the end, I had the most electoral votes and I won. My mother attempted to congratulate me using my real name, but I said, President Wallace asks that you clean this up, please. Mr. Vice President, please get wrestling on TV. Thank you. I didn't want to be a bad president, but my family was annoying. And I wanted to see how far my power could go.

My elementary school classroom was stocked with two sets of encyclopedias, and I was casual about looking up George Wallace in *World Book* and then *Britannica* during a study period. In one encyclopedia, there was a photo of Wallace on a stage with Richard Nixon. Wallace wore a white suit, he looked more like a preacher than a president. Nixon grinned and applauded. It looked like a lot of rotten stuff was happening down in Alabama.

As she was making our dinner on Tuesday night, my mother called me into the kitchen; she stood by the skillet and in a casual way she said, Hey, you don't brag on George Wallace at school or anything do you? My mother was a decent, hard-working Ohio-an. Without her support, I had nothing. I knew what she was worried about. Some of our neighbors were Black, including Ed-die Tolan from my father's bowling team. He watched TV at our house on college football Saturdays.

I said, No way, Mom. My friends would think that stuff's kinda lame.

She said, Your father just wants you kids to learn…about, you know, America.

I must've been a decent president. At the end of my week-long term, our family was having a dinner of fried chicken and mashed potatoes. My sister said she thought I was a real retard, president or not, and she was surprised the house hadn't burned down. My mother reported that she hadn't seen any Russian tanks crawling up High Street. My father had been drinking beer all afternoon, a celebration of a job interview he'd been able to procure for the following week as a sales clerk at JCPenney. The store manager was a friend of a friend, so the interview, my father said, was little more than a formality.

A couple of times he asked me what it felt like to be presi-dent. He said that he knew I could grow up to be a presi-dent…me, or my sister. I didn't know what to say to that; my sister and I were pretty bad students. I wanted to be like Denny McLain, the Detroit pitcher who bet on games with the mob. My sister had her heart set on twirling a baton in the high school band.

Once dinner was done, we got out *Landslide* and looked over the candidates we'd chosen the week before. We lived in a crappy house and in a crappy state. To me, it felt right to be upset about something. But I decided to lose on purpose; I could be a different candidate after that, somebody my mother wouldn't have to wring her hands over. When the game started, I tossed that dice and moved my photo of Wallace from place to place.

My sister kept calling me "President Hee Haw" and it started to get on my nerves. When I had to draw cards from the *Win Votes* or *Politics* stacks, I'd get good news. I could get on a plane and fly to different regions. I kept collecting electoral votes. My sister quit when I outbid her for California. At the end, it was close but I wound up with a few more electoral votes than my mother. She'd had a couple of beers by then and with a laugh announced she wanted a recount, and so my father and I added up the votes again. I'd won; of course, my parents had to abide by that. After the recount, my mother said, Fuck it, Dougie, I concede. I went out to watch TV, didn't order a clean-up of the table because my father was giving me an I-got-this look. I heard them talking, he got her laughing again.

JCPenney hired my father, and when he came downstairs to start his new job the following Friday, we all applauded. He wore a too-tight button-down shirt, a wide, yellow and brown striped necktie. If I'd been more on the ball I could've claimed that my administration was putting people back to work and so on. But despite the fuss we made, my father appeared tense and unhappy. His father had worked at U.S. Steel in Gary, Indiana, and my father had union jobs since he was nineteen years old. He was in danger of turning into a real candyass. He'd been out of work for something like five months already. He went in the next day, too, a Saturday, and after he got home, we all sat down to dinner. My father talked about a shipment of polyester leisure suits, said the manager wanted him to start wearing one to help sales. He had his choice of colors: cherry red, chocolate brown, sky blue. He looked right at me and said, And the first time you make fun of it, I'm getting one for you, too. He had a little of the devil in his eyes, so we could see he was only halfway joking.

I guessed we weren't going to be playing *Landslide,* but then my mother was telling my sister and me to clear the table and right after that she was opening the box and taking out the game board. My father stared at his photo of Humphrey. He said, I don't want this. I know all about Chappaquiddick, and I know that was wrong. I'd still rather be Teddy Kennedy. Any objections? He looked from my sister to me to my mother. Nobody said a word. We didn't have a photo, so for a player piece he wound up using a saltshaker.

My sister shocked everybody when she said, I want to be Patsy Mink! It sounded like a name on the marquee at The Sly Cheetah and my parents tried to appear patient. Then my sister was showing everyone a photocopy of a smiling, middle-aged woman with thick black hair. My sister said, Running for president! United States Representative from Hawaii. The school librarian helped me a little.

Even though the photo was a little blurry, I could see Patsy Mink had all these leis around her neck. It made me feel better just looking at that. My parents were pretty thrilled.

Also, they totally rigged the game that night. Every time either of them had a chance to steal votes, they took mine. My father used millions of votes to get tiny electoral states from me, like Rhode Island and Mississippi. I wound up with the lowest electoral count of anyone. I shrugged it off. On the whole, my family didn't ask for much. I'd have helped them if I really could've.

The Mink presidency began poorly. Instead of *All in the Family* or wrestling, my sister made us watch this dreary show called *Getting Together* with Bobby Sherman playing a songwriter or something. My father fell asleep and began to snore until my mother jiggled him. Huh, out of my way! he said and sat up fast. I guessed he'd been having a dream, maybe about running for president himself. His eyes blinked fast, then darted around the room and he said, Sorry, everybody. I really am. At nine-thirty we turned to *Mary Tyler Moore*, which was my mother's favorite show. No board-game president was going to mess with that. Then we kids had to go to bed.

During the middle of the week of her term, my sister fell on a patch of ice and chipped a tooth, and while she was at the dentist's office he said it looked like she'd need braces. The good news was that my father was employed and we probably could afford to make time payments. My sister worked the chipped tooth. She stayed home from school on Thursday, sat home all day watching soaps. As soon as I got home, she touched at her swollen lip with a wet rag and told me to bring her a Coke with ice. She tried for Friday, too, but my mother said no way. On Saturday, my father had to work late because the store was running a sale. My mother and sister and I wondered about *Landslide* but nobody seemed into it. It seemed obvious then that he'd been the only reason we'd played it in the first place.

His favorite team ever, the Detroit Red Wings, were on TV and my mother wanted us to be already tuned into that when he got home. She walked to the living room window a couple of times, maybe just to watch the snow falling. He didn't get home till after nine, and we were all looking in the direction of the living room doorway when he arrived there. When he shed his overcoat, we could see he'd gone with the cherry red leisure suit. His open-necked shirt had tumbleweeds in the pattern. Who's president this time? he said with a helpless smile.

Why, you are, my mother said.

He nodded, said, How'm I doing?

Red Wings three, Maple Leafs two, I said, trying to be helpful.

Without another word, he walked through the living room to our kitchen. My mother already had the sound low and she probably understood he was waiting for her now. I listened for the sound of a beer being cracked open but it was quiet out there. She left my sister and me to see about him. I could picture them sitting at the kitchen table. I heard them speaking in murmurs. He laughed and said, I was a great salesman when I wasn't a salesman, Alanna.

I'm tired of it, too, she said.

My sister and I glanced at one another. Neither of my parents spoke for a minute.

The next thing I heard my father say was, I'm going to give it all I can.

She said, That's all anyone can ask. I love you.

My eyes were on the TV again. The hockey game was in the third period; the Maple Leafs were on a power play. Right then, I felt terrible about everything but especially because I was such a bad student. My father had brought home this board game so we might get involved with politics and so my sister and I could take turns pretending to be the president. She'd chosen the happiest candidate and I'd gone with the angriest. What had we learned? Kids like us shouldn't be playing? I wasn't going to be the president someday; they said everybody grew up thinking they could be, but in my case, I knew it was for the best. I was some stupid kid living in a town a real president wouldn't be caught dead in. My parents stayed out in the kitchen, talking. It was the middle of winter in Ohio. The wind kept blowing against the windows.

Tower

Julian's ex Paula lived out in Fresno, California, and they were Facebook friends. He hadn't seen her in years. Their thirty-three-year-old daughter Tina lived an hour south of him, in Rockville. They'd swapped presents a few days before Christmas, while having lunch at the Chili's in Lafayette. Tina said on Christmas Day she'd be going to a party at a friend's house. The County Market was closed, so Julian didn't have to work. He told her he was just going to put his feet up, watch whatever sports games were on TV, get the day over with. He woke up Christmas morning with a hit of Reunite wine. He woke up most mornings that way.

Since she'd left him, Julian talked with Paula occasionally; the traditional calls came on their birthdays and New Year's Eve. On their recent New Year's Eve call, which took place in the evening Indiana-time, Paula mentioned Julian's lunch at Chili's with Tina. She said that Tina felt Julian was depressed, he seemed quite down. Julian pressed her for more information. She said, "Julian, she mentioned it. Tina said, 'Pop seems really down.'"

He said, "She didn't say that to me."

"Maybe she didn't want you to feel self-conscious."

"I'm…fine. I put on a good face for her… We always do."

"It's just something she said."

"I thought she seemed down, so I was acting like I wasn't. Look, it was gray outside. It was Christmas time."

"Well, maybe that…"

"When I asked about her painting, she changed the subject."

"You all need to get out of the goddamn Midwest."

"She should've said something to me. I'm fine. I could've explained that. Are things okay with you? How's the real estate business?"

"There's a lot of money out there, now that everything's deregulated." He thought she sighed. "I thought we went through that 'greed is good' phase. This country is for shit."

He wanted to cheer her up, make a point, so he said, "Supposed to snow six inches here tonight. I guess you can drive over to the Pacific any time..."

"I never had anything against the snow. I hear you're drinking again."

His mind scanned over the lunch he'd had with Tina; he hadn't ordered anything alcoholic. "Seasonal," he said. He didn't say anything else.

"Maybe I shouldn't have said anything. Don't tell Tina you know she told me. And, please, don't say anything about what I just told you."

"She's our daughter, Paula. We can talk about her."

"It's more important that she talks to us."

You mean you. He didn't bite, said, "Listen...happy New Year, okay?"

"Sure, Julian. You take care of yourself."

"You, too."

On New Year's morning, he awakened and went out to his kitchen, extracted a wine bottle from his refrigerator, removed the screwtop, and took a drink. He prepared himself for work. It wasn't any store holiday. Before he brushed his teeth, he had another swallow of wine. He dressed, pulled on his jacket. At the supermarket, he went to his office, closed the door, looked over spreadsheets. He surfed the web for some time; he read headlines and news articles but clicked out of them before getting too worked up. He checked out the *Trib*'s Arts & Entertainment page.

At ten, he took a break and called Tina, to wish her a happy New Year. Also, he told her he wanted to take a trip up to Chicago, to the Art Institute. A Manet exhibition had recently opened. Would she like to join him? This Saturday?

Tina said, "You like Manet, Pop?"

"You can explain to me why the paintings are so good."

She gave a faint-sounding laugh. "You know why they're good."

"Because they're hanging in a museum."

"Yeah, well, that's not the whole story. You really need somebody to explain it to you?"

"We haven't been there in years."

"No. You're right. Well, lemme check, okay? I'll check and I'll get back to you. You caught me a little off-guard."

"Happy New Year, sweetheart," he said. "It'll be a good one, I can feel it." He placed the phone on his desk, reached inside his laptop bag and took out a split of Reunite Bianco. Cheap, sweet wine. Before Thanksgiving, the local distributor's salesman had given him a case of Bianco fifths, a thank-you for all of County Market's business. The gesture wasn't legal, and the salesman didn't know Julian's history. Julian accepted the gift; prior to that, he hadn't had a drink in six months at least. He told himself he'd just drink through the holidays.

He drained the split in a matter of seconds. He kept cough drops in his bag and he chewed on a couple of those before heading out to the floor.

* * *

Julian and Paula had dreamed of different lives for themselves; they'd met in grad school at Purdue. She wanted to be an editor, live in New York. He felt certain he would be the next major Midwestern poet, follow in the footsteps of Sandburg, Levine. By the time Tina had reached her senior year of high school, the household was tense. It seemed as if no one could agree on anything. Concerning college, they felt it might be better if she stayed close to home, attended Purdue or IU. But then Tina was accepted into an arts program at Boston University, and after she moved away for school, he and Paula stayed together and tried to talk through their problems. Once, when Tina came home for fall break, she brought somebody with her, a blond guy named Curtis, a chem major. They joked about quitting college and traveling the world as tramps. The following summer, she took a See-the-USA road trip with her friend Marcy, and they stopped in Lafayette for a couple of days. At dinner, Tina announced she and Marcy were dating. Her parents envied their daughter's happiness, her freedom. After Tina's graduation, she went traveling in Europe with friends. Julian and Paula filed for divorce.

Paula had old college friends of her own who were living out in California and decided to try her luck there. Tina went for her master's degree at Virginia Commonwealth. She loved her classes and made friends. But somewhere along the way, she lost inspiration. She decided to come back to Indiana because that was where she'd once believed she was going to be a great painter. She'd make a living, get a job teaching art in Lafayette or Bloomington. She wanted to paint images of the Midwest. Tina couldn't get a job at a state university, so she wound up teaching at a community college in Rockville. She taught a full load of classes, mostly basic drawing courses. They got away with paying her next to nothing. She barely had time to do any of her own painting.

Julian couldn't help but go over the lunch at the Chili's in Lafayette: he'd bought Tina a down vest for Christmas and included a $250 Amazon gift card. She'd renewed two magazine subscriptions for him, *Smithsonian* and *American Scholar*, and presented him with a chocolate brown cardigan sweater. She ordered a garden salad and iced tea; she didn't drink, never cared for the stuff. He had tea, too, and chicken fingers. He'd tried to keep the discussion light, even when she started talking about Trump and McConnell and the destruction of democracy. He'd said to her, You have to live your life, sweetheart. The world is still full of wonderful things. She'd regarded him kindly. You look kinda tired, Pop, she had said that. I'm fine, he'd said. She favored him, had dark hair, brown eyes. He didn't say it, but he thought she looked tired, too.

The day after his New Year's call to her, Tina texted him: *read up on Manet exhibition, supposed to be amazing. i'm in. can meet you at the store on saturday.* He supposed she'd also called Paula and Paula had encouraged it. Maybe she asked Tina to talk to him about his drinking. That evening, he dialed Tina and they made plans. After this, even though he knew he shouldn't, he thought about calling Paula and telling her they were heading for the Art Institute on Saturday. He wouldn't call her because he'd been drinking. When he talked with Paula, he was wary of sounding nostalgic. They all wanted to live in the here and now; he was as aware of that as anyone could be.

On that Saturday morning, he went through his usual routine and though he was heading for the store, he didn't pull on the red vest all the employees had to wear, even the managers. The morning mist was so heavy he had to flip on his windshield wipers. He pictured the skyline of Chicago, the buildings he and Paula used to point out for Tina. Today, they'd see the Trump Tower, which hadn't been completed until after Tina had left Indiana. Back when the family had just been starting out, it had been the *Sun-Times* Building. Julian had always sort of hated the idea of the tower, especially when the city fathers had given in to Trump's demand that his name be spelled out in 20-foot letters on the side that faced the Chicago River.

Julian had an idea, an inspiration. By the time he reached the store, he was even feeling chipper. Margaret Grant, the twenty something assistant manager, had agreed to take over for him for the day, and she was already behind the desk in the manager's office when he arrived. He stood in the doorway of the office, said good morning, then asked if she'd head for the back and check to see if the Sara Lee delivery driver was unloading their order and, if so, could Julian have a word with him. Margaret's expression seemed uncertain, but she said of course and he stepped aside so she could pass. He closed the door, went to the desk and took out the four splits of Reunite he'd forgotten to remove from the day before. He worked the bottles into a pocket of his laptop case. By the time Margaret returned, he was in the produce section, and as she approached him he said, "Sara Lee delivers on Mondays. I remembered a second after you left…when you're fifty-five, make sure you aren't running a supermarket." Margaret smiled at him with patient, blue-green eyes. She was married to some guy who fixed motorcycles, was always broke. Julian said, "My daughter and I are going to Chicago today."

"You mentioned that."

"Well, I'm going to pick up a few things for our drive."

"I'll be in the office. That's okay, right?"

"Of course."

Julian was standing in the express line when he spotted Tina's grape-colored Honda Fit pulling onto the lot. By the time she stepped through the opening provided by the sliding glass doors, it was his turn to pay. She wore a dark, knee-length wool coat, jeans, boots, and an emerald-green beret. He held out $10 to Roderick, a checkout clerk. "Did you take out my discount?"

"Yes sir."

"Oh, I know you did. Thank you." He walked over to Tina carrying a plastic sack with two bottles of orange juice and two maple-iced donuts. She craned her neck forward so he could kiss her cheek. "Morning, sweetheart," he said.

"Hey, Pop."

Tina led the way outside. She stood by the driver's door of her Fit.

"You wanna drive?" he said.

"Get in," she said.

Julian owned a 200,000-mile Crown Vic, which had plenty of leg room. In the Honda, he sat with his laptop case wedged between his calves and the seat. "How's business?" Tina said, right after they'd darted up the ramp and onto the interstate.

"Little slower than usual during the holidays. I'm sure you had to cancel something for this. Didn't mess up your work schedule?"

She shrugged. "We're still on Christmas break. I can smell the...whatever on you. Jesus, Pop."

He glanced down at his hands. "It's fine." He cleared his throat. "Aim for downtown Chicago, Michigan Avenue."

"I know where we're going," she said.

They drove north on I-23 under a smoky gray sky; she had the radio on NPR, a story about voter suppression. He said, "Heard from your mother?"

"Sure. We talk."

They listened as a professor from Northwestern discussed voter turnout in recent national elections, that more than ninety million eligible voters had skipped participating. The professor said one logical conclusion was that a lot of people had simply given up on the idea of the government. "I got a surprise for us," he said. "Want me to tell you what it is?"

She glanced in his direction, a slender smile on her face. She had delicate features. "I can wait."

"Okay," he said. In the next moment, he said, "I want us to walk up Michigan Avenue, give the finger to the Trump Tower."

"You're kidding."

"Nope."

"That's hysterical."

He said, "I know you hate all this stuff that's going on. I know it bothers you."

"Said the man who carries a fifth in his pocket."

Actually, he had splits of wine in his laptop case—there wasn't a joke there, however. He said, "You have a future, you've worked hard."

She said, "You know when I'm talking about Trump or Pence or whoever...you know, they're disgusting, dangerous human beings. They happen to be running the country. I think anybody with an IQ over…" She'd taken her right hand from the wheel, turned the palm upward. She squinted in his direction.

"I'm your father," he said. "I don't want you to be unhappy."

"Everyone's unhappy."

"I know that," he said. "We're talking about you."

Wait, Wait, Don't Tell Me had begun. She turned up the volume a bit. Peter Sagal introduced the panel of comedians, and after a couple of minutes Julian and Tina were smiling. One panelist joked that a hundred years from now all his grandkids would get their degrees from Kardashian State.

Laughing, Julian said, "Poor things, such easy targets."

"I don't think the joke's on them," Tina said. "I read where Kim just bought a seven-forty-seven. The Trump Tower thing…you heard of the artist Ai Weiwei, you know who I'm talking about? He created this series, where he's basically the guy who gave the middle finger to the whole world. He's flipping off a Trump building, I think in New York. He also gives the finger to the Eiffel Tower, the Kremlin. The photos are simple: a guy's middle finger and the structure beyond it."

"Sounds like he's been reading his Dostoevsky."

"It does, actually."

"Maybe I read something about Ai Weiwei. Channeled it."

On the radio show, Fiona Apple was introduced as the musical guest. "Oh god, I love her," Tina said. She reached for the volume again. The highway stretched through the Fowler Ridge Wind Farms; white turbines stood in rows against the ice-blue sky all the way to the horizon. The sack he'd bought from the store sat on the console. He wolfed half of a maple donut, then held up the other half to her. She waved it off. He liked Fiona Apple, didn't know the song she was doing, and partway through Tina began to lightly snap her fingers. She sang, "Oh, if there was a better way to go, then it would find me. I can't help it, the road just rolls out behind me." He finished the donut, then wiped his hands together. He flashed back to when Tina was younger and the three of them were together, riding up here in that goddamn Taurus, a company car for when he'd been a supervisor for Nabisco. Paula would ride in the back so Tina could be up front, and he'd look in the rearview mirror just to enjoy his wife's pleased expression. He was still writing poetry in those days, mainly on the weekends, in the mornings, while Paula was still sleeping.

Past Gary, the sky turned milky, and once they made the 94 Express it began to snow. The flakes looked big, and they melted upon reaching the windshield. Tina set the wipers on intermittent. He felt she was driving a little too fast but chose not to say anything. The sky was dense with mist and snow, and he couldn't make out the skyline of the city until they spotted the exit signs for the museum. Tina had thought ahead, bought a parking ticket for a garage on Wabash that was half the price of a Grant Park garage.

After she'd switched off the Honda, he let her get out of the car first; while her back was turned, he swiped two splits from his laptop case, stuck them in the pocket of his coat. She turned up her collar. They walked together down a flight of steps and then were out on the sidewalks of Michigan Avenue. He pulled on a knit watch cap, said to her, "Is that enough hat?"

"I feel like wearing it today."

Up ahead, across Michigan, was a street-level skating rink; on a rise above the skate rental shop and restaurant stood Anish Kapoor's *Cloud Gate*, the curved, massive "silver bean" and its mirrored surface. Tina wanted to watch the skaters, so they crossed the street. They stood at the edge of the rink while the sound system played "Raise a Man" by Alicia Keys. Julian considered the stretched city skyline in the reflection of the sculpture. He and Paula, when they were just starting out together, had talked about moving up here, to the city. They should've done it.

They'd have starved at first, but that wouldn't have mattered. Tina had always been excited when they'd taken day trips up here. It was his fault; he was just a timid man and that was all, that was the only thing anyone who knew him would ever be able to recall. Tina stood profile to him and the snow fell on her beret and around her face.

"Hey," he said, "you just want to head right for the museum?"

"What?"

"Seems silly. Pointless. Protesting a building named for a terrible human being ruining an ignorant country."

She held her eyes on the rink. "Now I really want to do it," she said. "Let's do it."

"You sure?"

"Come on, Pop."

On their walk north up Michigan, he nodded to the other side of the street, the green and gold façade of the Carbide Building. "Never get tired of seeing that one," he said. His upbeat mood had disappeared, and he needed to fight back. He said, "The snow is really nice, isn't it?" They passed a Stan's Doughnuts, a Nutella Bar. A trio of blond female joggers in maroon sweat suits and white headbands went around them; at the end of the block, Julian and Tina wound up waiting for the light with the joggers. They ran in place, and the light stayed red too long for them. They sprinted across the street when the coast was clear.

Tina stood by him at the display window of the Blackhawks store. He marveled at the crisp-looking hockey sweaters. "How's the team this year?" she said.

After a moment, he said, "We're rebuilding."

The Trump Tower stood on the opposite side of the Chicago River. Julian's eyes moved upward, followed the building all the way to the spires. He felt the snowflakes on his face. They stood on the corner of Wacker and Michigan, waited for the light. This should not be here, he thought. This tower. The *Sun-*

Times had been here. He'd been younger then. Those twenty-foot high letters, T-R-U-M-P, they shouldn't be here, the city had fought that but in the end they'd relented. There shouldn't be a tribute to any man who, after the towers fell on 9/11, said he now owned the tallest building in New York City. Tina had her chin tucked as she crossed Michigan, he moved at her side. They passed the foot of the DuSable Bridge, wound up at the stone railing; right across the Chicago River stood the tower. Twenty yards further down the railing a family posed with the tower in the background; it looked like they'd stopped some passerby to take their photo. They had a child with them, but Julian guessed it didn't matter. "Here," he said, taking his phone from his pocket. "Make sure you get all of me." He turned, glanced past the riverwalk to the seafoam-green waters of the river. "Ready?" he said, and turned partway.

"Go," she said.

He flung his right arm in the air, middle finger extended.

"Hang on," she said. "Got it."

"Take another one."

"Okay...and one more...that's four of 'em."

He held his arm in the air for a few more seconds, then brought it down to his side again. He felt tears in the corners of his eyes, blinked them out. He stuck both hands in the pockets of his coat, turned, glanced in the direction of the family. They were heading up the sidewalk, away from him and Tina.

"Here," she said. "I want to do it." She held out his phone and went to the railing. She tugged at her beret and, with her back to him, held both arms in the air, middle fingers extended. He snapped one photo, then another.

"Great," he said.

At his side, she said, "Lemme see." He held the phone at chest level. Beyond her arms were the letters. "I tried to get the river in on yours," she said.

"Let's go," he said. "You're gonna get sick."

A man stood a few feet from them. Tall man, no hat, unshaven. "Y'all got any change?" he said.

"Change?" Julian said.

"Want me to take one of the both of you together?" He'd come from the direction where the family had been.

Julian had the singles left over from the supplies he'd bought at his store this morning. Four singles. The man accepted the money, held the modest wad of cash by his ear. "Bless you."

"You, too," Tina said.

Julian and Tina waited for the light and a seagull floated a foot above their heads, its wings spread. Then, it flapped off ahead of them. They walked back down Michigan in the falling snow, but it was as if Julian couldn't feel the cold. He was alive and his heart gave a little jump at the sight of the bronze lions on either side of the museum entrance, the Lions of Michigan Avenue. Inside, they shed their hats, batted snow from their sleeves. Beyond the information desk in the lobby were vertical banners hanging from the marble pillars.

<table>
<tr><td>E</td><td>A</td></tr>
<tr><td>D</td><td>G</td></tr>
<tr><td>O</td><td>E</td></tr>
<tr><td>U</td><td></td></tr>
<tr><td>A</td><td>O</td></tr>
<tr><td>R</td><td>F</td></tr>
<tr><td>D</td><td></td></tr>
<tr><td></td><td>B</td></tr>
<tr><td>M</td><td>E</td></tr>
<tr><td>A</td><td>A</td></tr>
<tr><td>N</td><td>U</td></tr>
<tr><td>E</td><td>T</td></tr>
<tr><td>T</td><td>Y</td></tr>
</table>

Julian reached for his wallet. The ticket counter was to their left; he held a credit card out to Tina, then excused himself. He found an empty stall in the men's room, where he downed one bottle, then the other. He washed his face, considered his appearance in the mirror. He hadn't needed the second bottle, he could've saved that. He felt the lighting in there was pretty harsh.

Tina waited for him near the admissions counter. "Here," she said, handing over his ticket and his credit card. "Go check your coat."

A minute later, he'd rejoined her. They walked up the curved staircase together, then through the glass doors of the Pritzger Gallery. They stood in front of the famous *A Bar at the Folies-Bergère,* displayed on the wall just inside the entrance. In the painting, a young, unsmiling woman stood behind a counter with corked bottles at her right hand. Behind her was a mirror, which reflected the bottles and a cafe full of people. There were people clustered around Julian and Tina and someone murmured, "Is that a mirror or is that café just really crowded?"

Tina left his side, but this was what she'd always done; even as a teen she'd peel off from her parents, do her own looking around. Julian examined the works in one gallery, then moved on to another. He studied *Return from the Ball,* which featured a well-dressed couple on a luxurious blue sofa. The man, who had a receding hairline, sat forward, speechless. The woman in the painting was upset, lying back with one arm thrown across her face. He moved on to other pieces, *Young Woman in a Garden,* then *Jeanne (Spring).* In a while, he spotted Tina standing before *The Brioche.* She'd always been partial to still lifes. He thought of the easel they'd bought her for her sixteenth birthday, the fruit Paula would buy, the "eating" bowl she'd set out so he wouldn't snack on something Tina intended to paint.

Julian took a seat on an otherwise empty marble bench, contemplated the Manet titled *The Café Concert.* A man in a top hat sat with his left forearm resting on the tip of a walking cane. The man looked distinguished, wore pince-nez glasses, had a graying mustache and chin-beard; he stared off at something, seemed preoccupied in his own thinking. The woman seated next to him had a full glass of beer in front of her; she sat back in her chair, looked rather bored. The man seemed to be aging well, dignified. Julian felt Manet might've been getting at that.

Tina joined him on the bench. She considered the painting. He said, "Thank you for coming here with me today."

"I shoulda thought of it myself. Manet."

In a museum voice, he said, "I used to think anything was possible."

"When you were like ten?"

He smiled, but didn't look in her direction. "I held on a little longer than that."

"Yeah, I guess I did, too." They sat for another minute. He listened to the creaking of the hardwood floors.

"Bless Manet," he said, in a murmur.

"What's that?"

He didn't answer.

She said, "I could use a little coffee. Food."

He felt there was a museum café somewhere on this floor, but he was content to let her lead the way. Over in the Modern Wing, they happened upon the Balcony Café; she said she wanted to treat, so he took an unoccupied table for two and waited. He sat with his head bowed, listening for the sounds—murmurs, footsteps—one would hear in any museum. Tina was back in a flash, placing two cups of coffee on the table. She left again, then brought back a plate that held a diagonally sliced vegetable roll. She held out half to him on a paper napkin. "I would've gotten more," she said. "But those prices."

"This is fine." The next thing he did was take a bite. He finished chewing and said, "I'm fine, you know that." With her index finger, she tapped at her two front teeth; he covered his mouth with his hand, used the nail of his small finger to work free whatever what was between his. "Got it?"

"Yep."

He shrugged. "I have a lot of things I'm looking forward to."

"What are you looking forward to, Pop?"

"Well…the Blackhawks. Crawford's playing better."

"Mmm-hmm."

"Spring will be here soon. What about you?"

"What?"

"Looking forward-wise."

"I'm thinking about Manet, actually. What he was thinking about when he painted. How he felt. You can't make yourself feel that way. You wake up every day that way. You have that feeling or you don't."

"How's your painting going? They're working you to death."

"Not really." She stirred her coffee. "I enjoy teaching. Things change, what you wanna do."

"No, they don't." For a moment, they were frowning at one another.

"You might have a point," she said. "But that's my concern."

He finished his roll, which took just two more bites. By reflex, he took his phone from the pocket of his shirt. No calls from the store. When he turned to phone to her, it held the image of her giving two middle fingers to the Trump Tower. She motioned for him to hand it over. He said, "I think we should post all the photos of you and me on the internet. We'll get fired by our employers. We'll be free."

She slid her finger across the screen. "These are good. Email me these, will ya?" She took her mug away from her mouth. "So, what will you do when you lose your job?"

"At County Market? Find another. They're supermarkets…they wouldn't fire me…you can't even see my face…I'm the best manager that store's had," he said with a laugh. "I'm twenty years older than everybody."

"Maybe all this is you trying to get fired. The drinking, I

mean."

He and Tina were still speaking in museum voices. "I'm not trying to get fired." He thought of Margaret Grant, seated at the manager's desk. He'd bought those Bianco splits right at the store, using his discount. He could've been more subtle about that. One day, if they did wind up letting him go, Julian would head back to AA. Meetings every day, some job on a night shift at a convenience store. "I'm not. Even so, I'd get by."

"Not that I blame you."

"Tina."

"When you got canned by Nabisco, Mom said…"

"Your mother… Look."

"I hang on to my job like it's the end of the world. I'd probably be better off without it, too. So, let's post these and get fired for a good reason. Here." She passed the phone back over to him and he placed it next to his wadded-up napkin. "Be on the news, like the lady who flipped off the motorcade in Virginia. Got fired, wound up getting elected to something."

"I just wanted to cheer you up a little bit."

"You know better. If I'm cross or down or whatever, so be it. You're my father, but that's insulting. Some people have good reason to be down." Her voice was quiet; he appreciated the fact she hated drama. She always had, for as far back as he could remember.

"Your mother…"

"She lives in California. She thought she could get away from all this…what's the word?"

"Your mother isn't happy?"

"You don't have to sound excited about it."

"I'm not. It always seems like she's got something going…her job."

"She had expectations when she went out there… I think that's changed. The word I was trying to think of was mediocrity."

He said, “Maybe she puts on a front for me. For whatever reason.”

“Pop, you can figure that out for yourself.”

“We just don’t want to make you feel worse.”

“Noted.”

“Really, want me to send you those pictures?”

“Yes, I do.”

“Right now.” As he did this, he said, “I’d live under an overpass, write poems on the insides of discarded cereal boxes. If I lost my job. I might be better off.”

“I’d visit you. Or join you.”

“Sent. Well, you wanna keep going?”

“Yeah, I do,” she said. “I read on the website about this six-hour film, this band singing the same song over and over. Probably downstairs.”

They bussed their own table, headed down a flight. At the entrance to the New Media gallery, they read the information panel: the film featured The National performing one song, “(A lot of) Sorrow,” during a six-hour session at MOMA.

“I think I heard about this,” Julian murmured.

He and Tina stepped inside the dark room, where there was one other patron, a guy sitting in the back row with his head bowed. On the screen, the band members, in their dark suits and white shirts, finished the song. At one point, while the lead singer was once more into the first lines, a stagehand stepped forward and taped a playlist to the floor near his feet. It said,

SORROW SORROW SORROW SORROW SORROW SORROW
SORROW SORROW SORROW SORROW SORROW SORROW
SORROW SORROW SORROW SORROW SORROW SORROW
SORROW SORROW SORROW SORROW SORROW SORROW
SORROW SORROW SORROW SORROW SORROW SORROW
SORROW SORROW SORROW SORROW SORROW SORROW
SORROW SORROW SORROW SORROW SORROW SORROW
SORROW SORROW SORROW SORROW SORROW SORROW
SORROW SORROW SORROW SORROW SORROW SORROW

SORROW SORROW SORROW SORROW SORROW SORROW
SORROW SORROW SORROW SORROW SORROW SORROW
SORROW SORROW SORROW SORROW SORROW SORROW
SORROW SORROW SORROW SORROW SORROW SORROW
SORROW SORROW SORROW SORROW SORROW SORROW
SORROW SORROW SORROW SORROW SORROW SORROW

The lead singer had to suppress a smile. He sang, "Sorrow found me when I was young. Sorrow waited, sorrow won."

They watched the group perform the song five times. Finally, Tina whispered to him, "Get the idea?" Outside the gallery, she read the synopsis again. "Heck, I was waiting for you to tell me you'd had enough."

"I liked the guy's voice. I liked it when the one guy taped…"

"Endurance Art. The idea is the performer does something to empty them out. Create exhaustion. Even suffering."

"Sounds great."

"I've read about Marina Abramovic, she's a pioneer. At one of her galleries, she sat in a chair, at a table for two, and faced anyone who wanted to sit across from her. She wouldn't speak. She would just keep her eyes on that person. Of course, the person would get tired. She sat there for eight hours straight. She has a method for concentrating, breathing."

"For breathing?"

"The idea is you become aware of your breathing. You become more aware of your space. The things around you." They'd entered an American gallery, the walls holding color fields by Ellsworth Kelly. Tina drifted into another room, he stood before one of Kelly's panels, the green; then he moved on to the red. He stepped into the room where she'd gone, but Tina wasn't there. He went from a Sargent to a Glackens, then an O'Keefe. He took a bench in front of Mary Cassat's *The Child's Bath*. A child sat on the lap of a woman in a long, striped robe, the two of them looking down at the bowl of water the child's feet were bathing in. Paula had always loved that one. It was impossible to be here and not think of her.

He stepped into another room: works by Inness and Homer. He stood before *Zapata* by José Clemente Orozco: a revolutionary standing in the doorway of a peasant hut, where a knife had been drawn on him. The figure represented Emiliano Zapata, there to help the peasants, who were explicably suspicious of everyone. The work was in the American gallery because Orozco had come to America to escape retribution for his works of the ruling class in Mexico. A great painting, he was just now appreciating that.

He returned to the Kelly gallery. While standing before an orange panel, he texted Tina, *where?* and she texted back *first floor, Japanese prints.* That's where he found her, in front of a six-panel screen, *Flowering Cherry and Autumn Maples with Poem Slips,* by Tosa Mitsuoki. Pieces of paper, poems, hung from the limbs of the maple trees. In these panels, the poems were the only evidence of human life. She stood with her fingers knitted together; he remained a few steps behind her. He waited for her to turn, drift in his direction. Which she did. "It's amazing how simple this is," she said.

He felt she was referring to the Mitsuoki, but for some reason didn't want her to clarify it. "Right."

"A high note for sure… I guess we probably ought to get going, Pop. Get back, start preparing for classes."

"Sure."

"Holidays are about done."

"I know."

He walked with her through the gallery and out to the lobby of the first floor. It seemed twice as crowded as when they'd entered. "Want something from the gift shop?" he said.

"No. This has been really nice, Pop."

He went to get their coats. Tina accepted hers, placed the beret atop her head once they were outside. In the falling snow, they faced Michigan Avenue, moved down the steps of the entrance. They had the lions on either side of them. He could not help but glance up the street, in the direction of the river. The sky looked as hard as steel and the temperature had dropped. It changed his mood, looking in that direction, and he thought of the two splits he had tucked away in his laptop case in the car. But he told himself he wasn't going to have another drink, not until he was back in his own apartment.

They sat in traffic on Lake Shore Drive while the Fit's wipers erased the snowflakes. They listened to the weekend edition of *The Takeaway* with Tanzina Vega. Tina followed the signs for the 94 Express.

"I've had half a veggie roll all day," she said, once they'd crossed back into Indiana. "I'm starving."

"We have donuts," he said. He reached into the sack, took out another maple, and when she waved it off he took a bite, then another.

"I'm thinking of something really bad. Maybe I'm reverting back to childhood. Fish sandwich and fries from McD's."

"I'm in." He finished the donut, folded the top of the sack, set it on the console. He said, "Sugar helps with drinking, cutting down on it." He'd just tossed that out there. More than anything, he wanted her not to worry. He had icing on the tips of his fingers and licked at them. He said, "I know the employees can smell it on me. The wine. I can only guess what they think."

"I think about my job," Tina said. "Why I hang on to it. In a way, it feels like I haven't given up." She cut her eyes in his direction.

"I haven't given up." Julian glanced down at his hands, then rubbed his palms together. "Hell, I think the kids who work for me feel sorry for me. I don't want anyone to feel sorry for me. I've had my chances. I'll have others."

"I will, too."

"I don't like my job. But I'm okay. I still come up with good ideas. Like today. I'd love some fries, actually. A freaking Big Mac."

"You got it."

The gray sky in front of them now held azure patches at the horizon. He wondered if something had been accomplished, if at the very least each of them could hold a bright outlook when the conditions were right. In a matter of minutes, they'd pulled off the interstate and Tina had them parked near the side door of a McDonald's. "I got it," she said. Once she was inside, he got out of the car and started pacing back and forth behind the bumper. The wine splits were still in the laptop case.

"Pop?" Tina said, back at the driver's side door of her Honda. "You ready?" He couldn't say how much time had passed.

"Right away," Julian said and went for the passenger side. Inside the car, she held over the tray of drinks and the sack of food. "The fish is me, the Big Mac is you. We each have and fries and ice waters. You okay over there?"

He removed sandwiches from the sack. "Yeah. Watch out for the tartar sauce, they always put a ton of that on the fish. I don't know why. Here." She was backing up the car. "Want me to scrape some off?"

"Just use a fry or something."

"They put napkins in here."

"Lemme get going before you hand it over."

They'd been on the interstate a minute, riding in the quiet of the Honda. He presented her with the fish sandwich, the wrapper opened so she could have a bite. "Thank you, sir," she said.

She had her lights on, twilight had arrived. He began to feel cheerful; another moment of crisis had passed. He swallowed a fry and said, "I don't live in the past or anything, if that's what you're thinking."

"You're full of big statements today."

"Perhaps I'm turning into a great philosopher."

"I wasn't thinking about you and the past right this second."

"Well, what then?"

"The stuff we saw today. Letting it all sink in. But, I'm not sure I buy that."

"The past?"

"You mean to say you wouldn't want it all to be the way it was, when you and Mom were together?"

"I didn't say that," he said. "I just said I don't live there."

"No," she said. "I don't think you do. I don't think either of us do." Her voice was light, and what she'd said almost sounded pretty. But it hurt to acknowledge it. He knew it hurt her to say it. The snow had ended by now, though she still had the wipers set to intermittent.

Julian said, "I thought the museum was particularly good today." It might've sounded like he was referring to a performer or an athlete, but he felt she knew what he meant. He took another bite of his Big Mac; the bun tasted stale, which he hadn't noticed. He cleared his throat. "Don't tell your mother you enjoyed it too much, though. It'll make her think we don't miss her."

Tina took a sip from her soda. "I'll tell her we talked about her."

"That is accurate." Julian had the idea then about taking out his phone, holding up the pictures they'd taken today, something to further his case that he didn't live in the past. But he decided against it. He reached for the power button on her radio, tapped it. Opera. "Okay?" he said.

"Yes."

They came to the wind-farm turbines, passing row after row. Julian listened to the opera, tried to understand. Intermission arrived. The broadcaster said, "Stay tuned, soon we will rejoin Aaron Copland's *The Tender Land*, performed by the Chelsea Opera." Julian finished his meal. He accepted the fish sandwich wrapper from Tina, stuffed it all in the bag. He leaned back, listened, wanted to follow what was happening. Against the mauve-colored sky were the silhouettes of the turbines and their turning blades. Finally, he dozed off.

He gave a snort as he awakened, then looked right to Tina. "Want me to drive?"

"We're almost there."

"What's happening in the..." He nodded to the radio.

"I think the guy's about to leave the woman, Laurie, high and dry. Maybe she'll be stuck on the farm forever. Lemme see if I can figure it out." In a few minutes, she said, "Yep, he left her."

"I didn't understand a word."

"I'm guessing. It was the nineteen-fifties."

The County Market was open till eight on Saturdays, and the lights inside the store were illuminated when they pulled onto the lot. "Need anything?" he said. "I get a discount."

She thought about it for a moment, said, "I'm okay."

"Are you sure? I get twenty percent..."

"I'll go shopping tomorrow."

"Come on, get it done. Be here now."

They went in together. She started by pushing her cart through produce and he went to check the Customer Service counter, which was manned by Cleo, a kid just out of SIU. Cleo reported that Margaret's husband had dropped by on his Harley and taken her to dinner. It had been a while ago; he said she said she'd be back in time for closing. Cleo looked sheepish, like he'd said too much, but Julian said, "Kinda cold to be riding around on a motorcycle."

"Maybe they didn't have far to go."

"Get back to work," he said, even though there weren't any customers around.

Still in his coat, Julian sat down behind the desk in his office. He'd traded days off with Margaret, so he'd be back in here tomorrow. He knew he'd sit up and drink tonight, watch the Blackhawks if they were on. Through the office window he could see Tina guiding her cart through the bread aisle and he stood then, turned off the lights and locked the door behind him. Julian went back to Customer Service, told Cleo not to tell Margaret he'd been here. Cleo nodded, but Julian knew better, so he said, "Do it this way. Tell her not to worry about it."

He caught up to Tina, saw she had a few things in the cart; she could've done with just a hand-carrier. "That's it?" he said. "I guess we don't have a great variety. We do have whole wheat rolls on sale."

"That's all right. I'm good, I think this is it."

"Here." He reached for the handle, began to steer the cart for the line of registers. "I got it." He paid using his discount and bought a reusable bag for the groceries to go in. He walked Tina out to her car, held the bag over to her, and she kissed his cheek.

"Keep trying, Pop. That's all we got."

"You're a wonderful daughter," he said.

She gave his shoulder a squeeze. Then, she got in her Honda, put it in reverse, and backed out of the parking slot. He stood out there for a minute after her car had turned onto the ramp heading south.

When Julian got back to his apartment, the first thing he did was open the refrigerator and take out the chilled bottle of Bianco, gulped like it was Gatorade. He sat at the kitchen table with the bottle in front of him. It almost felt as if he were celebrating. It was important to have days like this; this was what he could hope for. He loved Tina and he'd loved her mother. He'd taken off his jacket, decided to listen to the hockey game on the radio while sitting at his kitchen table. He went through the photos of the tower. He imagined them framed, displayed on the wall of a museum. *America: A Day with My Daughter.* A contribution at last! In a while, he felt his shoulders sag. He needed to get up in the morning.

Midway through the third period, the Blackhawks were trailing the Canadiens, another rebuilding club, 4-1. He switched off the radio. His phone vibrated; a text from Tina: *get home okay?*

He thought about what to text back, to thank her for her

company and her patience. Say they ought to do this more often. He'd been drinking. He thought about offering a bit of fatherly advice: Listen, whatever you do, just don't turn out like I did! Make her smile. Though if she didn't see it as a joke, it might ruin everything. Besides, she'd only asked if he'd made it back to his place.

of course, he wrote. He pressed Send.

Hialeah

In addition to being a lifelong gambler, my father fancied himself something of a horse-racing historian. He owned books about racing's rich past, and he studied them primarily when we were on the road or when he was between jobs. He occasionally interrupted my homework if there was something he wanted me to see, and I loved any picture of a race on a muddy track, the way the photo held the slop-covered, hard-running horses in place. One Christmas, he bought me a used hardcover book called *A History of Horse Racing in America*. It must've been on sale because the binding was worn and the cover was put on backwards; when you opened it, you were already at the end. And the pages were upside down. You just had to flip the whole thing over and then it all made sense.

At one point in our lives, we lived in Ybor City, right on the outskirts of Tampa. Prior to that, we'd been in Birmingham, Alabama, which had been an unlucky place. It was my mother's idea that we try a new town and they decided on a place close to Tampa, where there was a horse track, something my father preferred to the dogs, which was all there'd been in Birmingham. What I mean by this is that we knew he would never quit gambling. It might've been what my mother liked about him the most. After we moved to Tampa, things began to look up. My father found a job as a parking valet at Burgundy's Italian Restaurant. She found work, too, helped take inventory at an office supply warehouse. She rode the bus to work; they both did. Then, out of nowhere, he had one of the biggest scores of my childhood. My father bet $600 to win on some 18–1 shot named Bowl Game that came in at Tampa Bay Downs. A $600 bet was huge for us, so my father had been either very confident or very desperate. With part of the proceeds, he bought an old goat of a car, a maroon Eldorado, from an ex-jockey named Sandy Paultz.

My parents, whose names were Lyle and Eleanor Moynahan, split up on any number of occasions, and not long after he got rid of the Eldo he left again. He went to Jacksonville, wound up as a waiter at a popular Mexican restaurant. He liked those jobs that involved tips. From Jacksonville, he called for us to join him, and after a while we did. When I was seventeen, I flew the coop myself, decided to join a horse stable heading for Louisville, and this was where my own complications began. I didn't see my parents as much after that, though I guessed they settled down some. For years, they would stay together in a little apartment in St. Augustine, where each of them worked at jobs waiting tables. Just south of there happened to be a simulcast parlor where my father could bet on horse races from across the country.

About two weeks after he'd driven the Eldo home for the first time, he arrived at our apartment right after eleven, which was usual. He wore his unbuttoned black valet vest, and my mother and I were sitting on the couch, watching TV: David Letterman talking with Isabella Rossellini. I was almost thirteen and the couch was also a fold-out bed, where I slept. My mother liked for him to see that we'd both waited up...that we were waiting. Maybe for him to see that he was worth waiting for. He did need to be reassured of so many things, though I have learned this is not exceptional with gamblers.

My father closed the door and stood just inside our apartment. "Go get your book, Denny," he said. "Your history."

I was already on my feet. I knew what he meant. I used their room for studying, when I studied. The TV was too big a distraction, and when my mother got home from work, she liked to have a drink and watch her shows. When I returned, my parents had seated themselves at the small table near the kitchenette. There were just two chairs and that was fine; when I placed the racing-history book in front of my father, I stood at his shoulder.

His mind must've been buzzing because he forgot the way the cover of the book went; he opened it, and for a second he seemed bewildered. I was about to say something when he turned it around.

"What do the two of you know about Hialeah?" he said. He was like a trying-to-sound-casual-but-I-know-you-did-it TV detective, and my mother's eyes went to me for a second.

"Palm trees?" she said.

He turned pages. "Those are everywhere," he said. My mother and my father were both tall, unique-looking people. Her hair was thick and kinky and she had clay-colored skin. She'd grown up in Oklahoma and had learned how to drive a tractor at age twelve. My father was a slender man with a tall forehead that featured wavy, faint wrinkles. He had a long nose and a small mouth and he rarely looked comfortable.

"It's in Miami. Citation ran there," I said. "Spectacular Bid won the Flamingo Stakes by twelve lengths in 1979."

Finally, he had what he was looking for. "Here," he said, and he guided the book in her direction. "Joe Widener started this track up in 1932, right in the teeth of the Depression. Made all his money investing in the Philadelphia streetcar system. Mass transit. He built Hialeah because he wanted people to be optimistic about the future."

My mother watched him in her ready-to-boil way. But the thing was, she rarely lost her temper. "Why don't you just tell me what's going on?" she said. She kept her arms folded on the table, wouldn't reach for the book.

I couldn't see his whole face, just part of his profile. "All right," he said. "Bowl Game is running at Hialeah on Friday. We're gonna go watch him."

"All right," I said.

Her eyes went from me to him. "And?"

"Well, we'll bet him."

"Bet what?"

"Let me explain something to you about Hialeah, Ellie." He touched the tabletop with the tip of his index finger. "This time next year, it'll be closed. Look at these pictures. Can you believe that? It's crazy."

My mother's eyes found the book. He had it opened to a photo of the great Calumet Farm racer Coaltown. The sun shimmered off the colt's black coat as he was frozen forever just a few strides from the finish line in the Everglades Handicap.

I knew plenty about Hialeah myself. The horses raced against a backdrop of palm trees, and in the stands fans dressed sharp and looked pretty elated about their places in the world. Everyone was a winner. The pictures from there sometimes included the flamingos that lived right in the infield. They were odd-looking, peaceful birds who were oblivious to the hard-running horses and the cheering crowds.

"Bowl Game running there, it's an omen," he said. "I've always wanted to see this place. Look at how beautiful it all is. All we hit are the crap tracks. This'll be gone next year. This particular chance." Her expression weakened a bit. "The glory of a great racetrack."

I said, "I want to go."

Her eyes went to me, then back to him, then to me and to him again. "What're you asking me?" she said.

"I won't go if you don't ride along," he said.

"It would be good for me to see a historical place," I said.

"I don't mind it here," she said, in a quiet way. "If the horse loses…"

He cleared his throat; his eyes went to the book. He reached for it, flipped some pages. "This was published in 1984," he said. "It doesn't really talk about what's happened to Hialeah of late. See, horse racing is dying out. It's old fashioned." At this point, I supposed he was talking to me. He turned more pages and said, "The modern world needs to be entertained every second. The guy who eventually took over the track from Widener, he didn't pay attention to that. If you can't see what's changing in the world, you lose out. Now, the track is closing. Soon. They'll be running the dogs there before you know it. It'll be worse than Birmingham. The guy who owns the place now, he isn't a man of his time."

In a measured way, my mother said, "That's nothing to worry about, Lyle."

"Well, I do," he said.

I said, "If you take me, I swear to god I will get straight A's this term. I absolutely swear."

My mother looked in my direction and my father turned, too. It was a lie; we all knew it.

She simply shook her head. "So dramatic." She glanced out to the living-room area, let her eyes tour around. It was difficult to say precisely what she was thinking about. My mother seemed cool and focused. "I'm not crazy about counting boxes of rubber bands," she said. "If, in fact, this is the point you're trying to make. But do you have to bet everything?" He didn't answer, and then she sniffed and looked around the living room again. "What I wonder about more than anything is why you're asking me." When she steered her glance his way again, her eyes seemed to be smiling. But then they weren't. "I don't know why you need my approval."

"I can do this," he said. He shrugged. "I already know that you approve."

I thought she might get up and walk over to a window and look out at the street. "Any chance this horse can win?" she said, just flicking her fingers at a crumb or something on an open page of the book.

My father didn't answer, not for a minute. But it was clear he needed to. His eyes were on the table top when he said, "The problem is the horse could win and we'd miss out on it. On a big hit. At this world-famous racetrack that's not even going to be around for much longer. I don't really think there's much choice, do you, El?"

My mother took in one long breath, then another. "I just don't want the drama, okay, Lyle? That's the one goddamn thing I do not want." Her voice was steady. "And you, promising something." I just gave her a quick shrug. She looked at him again. "No drama, do you hear me? Plus, a hotel on the beach."

The book was between them, at the center of the table. I was getting excited and wanted to look at the pages about Hialeah again. But it didn't seem to be the right time for that.

Finally, my mother said, "I can fix you something. Are you hungry?"

He nodded. He said, "I'll take anything you make."

* * *

My parents picked me up from school after classes on that Thursday afternoon—they'd both called in sick to their jobs—and once we were on the interstate, my father eased the Eldo into the right lane and there we stayed while the sun floated towards the western horizon. At one point, my father leaned back in his seat, set his hand atop my mother's headrest. He said, "Oh, goddamn, here..." He reached for a folded newspaper sticking up between the seats. "Tomorrow's edition." It was a *Daily Racing Form*. "What about tomorrow's results, they going to be in there, Denny? Man, think about that. You'd be the only one in the world who would have them, too." I sat back, opened the thing, leafed through the pages for Hialeah. "Think of that," he said.

I didn't like it when he talked to me like I was a baby. I said, "This car's a tub, old man."

"A has-been jockey sold it to me." His voice a quiet laugh. "Old Sandy. He was the one who gave me the tip on Bowl Game. I park his car when he comes to the restaurant. He said if the horse won I'd have to buy this car from him. Imagine that, some goddamn jockey...telling me...he said, 'Just don't take it too far and it'll run to the end of time.' I got it for free if you're looking at this thing a certain way." His voice had this vacancy to it, like he couldn't help anything at all. "Your mom thinks it's just gonna come apart."

"I didn't use those exact words," my mother said. She didn't appear to be in a poor mood, but she certainly didn't seem to be someone on her way to bet on a jet-fast runner. Bowl Game was entered for the third race tomorrow. The handicapper's notes said, *Up from the bushes...would need a career best. Proceed with caution.* None of the five expert handicappers had Bowl Game listed in their top three choices. I felt like asking him about it, but my father was never too interested in any details that didn't support his current point of view. He was illuminated in the yellow-green light of the sun, and now and then a car went schooowee-yow as it whooshed by the Eldo. I folded up the paper and thought about what Miami would look like at night, if we would have the chance to take a speedboat ride. I wanted to go deep-sea fishing, that was another thing.

We reached the outskirts of the city after the sunlight was gone. First came illuminated seaside motels with names like The Swordfish Inn or Seashell Arms; the tight line of lighted rooms at The Teal Mermaid made me think of a left-behind train car. Casablanca, Silver Surf, Ocean View, Gold-A-Coast; places with exterior decorations that included splashy fountains, golden panther statues, martini neons. We passed strip malls, restaurants, apartment buildings with wafer-stacked floors. One empty lot featured a fifty-foot-high billboard, a spotlighted mural of the apartment building that somebody dreamed would be there soon. Silhouettes of palm trees lined an emptier expanse of highway. On the right appeared an inlet waterway with two huge yachts moored to a tiny dock, floodlights sitting in a small stretch of grass, hitting their hulls, making them seem like the tips of glaciers.

"The Beau Rivage," my mother said, sticking her arm forward, twitching the end of her index finger. "Pull in, Lyle, it's right up there. That's where I want to stay." Just a block ahead was the pillbox shape of the Beau Rivage Hotel, the words in cursive—blue neon—above the entrance. We wheeled into the parking lot, drove to where the sign pointed, stopped right in front. At the top of the steps, a bronze fountain splashed sky-blue water at the ankles of a life-sized sculpture…a god in a toga. A young, blond-haired guy in a mustard-colored jacket appeared at the driver's side of the Eldo and my father lowered his window.

"How far is Hialeah from here?" my father said.

The question changed something in the valet's helpful expression. His eyes went along the car, found me. "Coupla miles," the guy said with a smile in my direction. He said, "I don't think they race at night though, sir."

"I know when they race, son," my father said in this perfect way. Then, he turned slowly, looked at my mother. "This'll be fine," he said.

He wound up getting us a suite on the second-highest floor. He forked over four $50 bills and appeared somewhat stunned after receiving the key from the smiling desk manager. We rode the elevator upward, and it turned out our room had a huge panoramic window that held the downtown of Miami in the distance. The skyline of the city was a dazzling collection of angles. I put both hands on a section of the window pane. When I turned to see if my parents were watching, they seemed surprised about something, though it wasn't as if they were in some kind of romantic embrace. They were standing a few feet apart from one another.

My father and I carried the couch over to the big window so I could fall asleep there. My mother fretted a little, she thought I might go sleepwalking, but then my father tapped soundly on the window with a knuckle, said, "These things are reinforced. He'd have to take a running jump to knock it out. You're not going to do that tonight, are you?"

"I don't know," she said.

"Let him be close to it if he wants."

When I opened my eyes the following morning, my father stood right behind the couch and his focus was on that big window. The front of him was blanketed in a soft, canary-colored light and he stood there with his arms crossed, just watching, though I couldn't tell what he was interested in. He seemed holy, he was bathed in that kind of light. When I looked to the window, I had to squint.

"Hey, Dad," I said, right as he looked down at me.

"She's getting dressed...she wants to talk me out of it now." His jaw muscles knotted, then relaxed. "We shouldn't have come to this hotel. This is a bet of a lifetime, we need to stay focused. If we were staying in a motel, we wouldn't even be having this discussion. This play should matter, it ought to change something...shouldn't it? Do you ever think of a miracle, what that might constitute? My problem, or so it seems, is that I believe one is out there. Why do I think this way? What happens if this horse wins and we don't play it? It's a fortune lost right there. It eats at you forever, something like that." He stared at the shining sky. "I'd rather lose."

He wasn't talking to me, I knew that, but it suddenly seemed as if what he was saying was all that I knew for sure. This was a gambling trip, something I had been on with them before. Delta Downs in Louisiana, Oaklawn Park in Hot Springs, Remington Park in Oklahoma City. It certainly was unlike my mother to get cold feet, so maybe it had to do with this hotel. I knew she stepped into the room because he turned his head. "Get in the bedroom and get dressed," she said.

"Morning," I said when I brushed by her, and after I reached their bedroom, I closed the door. A clean pair of jeans and a rugby shirt were laid out for me on the bed, which she'd already made. It was just a force of habit.

When I walked out into the little living room again, my mother was seated at the couch facing the big window. She sat at one end of the couch, so I went over and took the other end and she didn't change what she was doing, which was just letting her eyes find different things beyond the glass. My mother had broken her nose when she was a child and there was a crooked place right between her gray eyes. Her coal-colored hair was pushed away from her face by a couple of barrettes. "I did try," she said. "He says I'm losing my edge. I'm giving up. That's really funny." To our left was the blue-gray Atlantic Ocean. A wiggly, vanilla-colored strip of beach. Back in Ybor City we had the Gulf nearby, so it wasn't like this was something new, this long, empty horizon. Last night, with the city buzzing at the other side of the window, I barely even noticed the water was there. "I don't care about big things anymore," she said, and at this I turned, but couldn't think of anything else to say. I couldn't tell if this was the truth or simply a response to a charge leveled against her by my father. They hadn't been arguing last night, at least not loudly. "I really don't," she said and then she lowered her eyes, considered her folded hands. "What do you want?" she said, like I was sitting on the couch for a particular reason.

To cheer her up a little, I said, "I could be in charge of Miami. I'd like to sit up here and have ten phones. I could give you any job you wanted."

"You'd make your mother work?"

"Well, yes, you would have to work for me. But just for me. It'd be all right."

"You sound exactly like him." She smiled quick, let it go. Then, she nodded, lifted her chin upward. "Does this horse have a chance today?" She knew how to read the *Racing Form*, so she might've been interested in something else.

"I don't know." I wanted to impress her somehow, so I said, "I probably wouldn't bet it."

"You shouldn't have opinions like this," she said. *You asked me,* I thought. I didn't say anything because it was always better when they weren't worrying about what I was learning. "When you grow up, get with someone who won't put up with what I do."

I thought, *Why would I do that?*

In a while, she said, "This is what I know now. I don't have a model life." My mother was not a complainer so it was hard to tell exactly what she was thinking about.

"I could work for you," I said. "But I would want something good. Like I could be in charge of all the Nathan'ses."

"But you couldn't eat Nathan's every day."

"See, already you're interfering," I said, trying to make my gripe sound authentic.

The door to our suite opened and my mother and I turned. After he closed it again, my father stood in place for a moment. Then he strode over to the couch and stopped a few steps from where he'd stood when I awakened. His hair was blown back and blasts of sand were stuck to the shins of his khakis. "I have to do it, El," he said.

"I know," she said.

"Okay," he said. "We gotta get going."

"Get him something to eat. And not just concession food."

"We'll live like kings."

He didn't wait a moment longer, walked right for their bedroom. My mother made half a fist, examined her nails like a man does. When she glanced my way again, she squinted as if I had just appeared, or she had noticed something different about me. "You're not eating Nathan's onion rings every day," she said. "No way."

"I wouldn't eat them every day," I said. "God."

"Damn straight you wouldn't," she said.

* * *

When my mother and I stepped through the opened glass doors of the hotel entrance, we were greeted with sweet-smelling tropical air. Beyond the bottom of the steps the Eldo gasped, but my father gave it some gas and kept grinning at us. His window was down and his expression dimmed as my mother, without a word, strode ahead of me. She leaned into the driver's window and straightened his collar. A horn honked behind us and my mother stepped back, nodded at him, then motioned for me to get into the car. By the time I was in the front seat, she was near the entrance of the hotel again, waving from beyond the fountain. My father got us rolling, but even when his eyes were on the highway, looking straight ahead, it seemed as if he was still seeing the entrance of the Beau Rivage. He didn't say anything and I didn't ask and I just hoped she wasn't leaving us for good. At least we had her suitcase in the trunk.

Hialeah was not far, just a few minutes away, and the entrance to the track was a road surrounded on both sides by fifty-foot-high palm trees. Their trunks curved and their fronds waved down. They seemed sorrowful to me. A huge, ivy-covered clubhouse stood in the distance.

My father nosed the Eldo close to a fence that separated the lot from the outside rail of the racing oval, then switched off the engine. The Hialeah flamingos and their pod-like bodies, stick legs, and hook-shaped necks were assembled at one corner of the metallic-blue infield lake. Now that I was here, it seemed even more peculiar that a home for flamingos would be at a lake that was inside a racetrack oval that was itself inside a big city. I said, "Why are those birds here, anyway?" I was hungry and guessed I sounded cross or something because he turned my way.

"Goddamnit," he said, though his voice was quiet. Then, he just put his hands on the wheel and looked at the windshield. "This is their sanctuary," he said. "Right?"

"It's weird, though."

He shook his head at something, said, "No, not at all. Tell me what a sanctuary is. What it means."

I just shrugged when he looked at me. "I could."

His eyes were on the windshield again when he said, "I go to bed at night knowing you're being raised right." His voice was a bit thin and I didn't know what to say. I was like every other kid out there, I wanted the horses we bet on to win. "We could just sit here," he said.

"I want to stay at the hotel," I said. That surprised him. "We can stay if he wins, right?"

"You got it," he said. He seemed to be thinking about it; by this I mean he appeared to be picturing something. "That's all I'm trying to accomplish here. I have about eight thousand dollars right now." He reached over, bumped his fist against the glove compartment, and the flap fell open. There were a few stacks of bills in there. He took them all out at once, with a single grab. "We could spend a month at the Beau Rivage. But then what would we do? An hour from now, I could have a hundred grand." Suddenly, he reached up and rubbed his free hand over his face. When he brought it down, he looked at me and his expression surprised me because he seemed exhausted. "I'm alive," he said. "That's the point. How about you kid, you alive today?"

"Sure," I said.

"Well," he said. "Are you coming?" His voice was as if this was what we had been talking about all along. He elbowed open his door. I walked at my father's side. He draped his arm across my back just for a moment, then took it away again. It was sunny and the bottoms of my sneakers felt warm on the asphalt.

My father produced a bread-slice-thick roll of $50 bills in one hand. He pulled off the one on top, held it over, said, "Pay for us to get in, hang on to the change." He looked at my face a second longer. He said, "Here, take another."

I just held out one $50 bill as we approached a turnstile, where a round-backed ticket taker sat on a tall stool. He didn't seem too far from being a flamingo himself. I waved my finger in the air, indicated to my father and me, and then I accepted the change, stuck it right into my pocket. The ground floor approaching the clubhouse was smooth cement painted a shiny gray, and the few gamblers there seemed to have come straight from wherever they'd last slept. Their shirts were out, unbuttoned. Some heads of hair were a little berserk. They were standing well-spaced from one another, each man by himself, and it made me think of the losing side of a chessboard.

My father nudged me. "I want you to see this," he said. He strode in the direction of a line of betting windows and stopped ten yards from them, stuck his hands on his hips. Overall, I couldn't tell if he was savoring the moment or trying to maintain his nerve. He walked for a window, announced his bet, and collected the tickets. He handed me one and said, "Here." I looked up at him then and he said, "If it loses, tear it up. Don't keep reminders. I'm ready for a drink now. Get out there, wait for me." The asphalt apron between the stands and outer rail of the homestretch was covered in sunlight. Nothing else out there but empty benches.

Out from the cover of the stands, I liked how the sun felt. I was excited to be there and wanted to feel free and wild myself. For a second, I thought of what the valet had said to us the day before, about when they raced, and that we were here on the wrong day. I was used to seeing empty stands at other tracks, but those were lousy tracks in small towns.

For lunch, I wound up getting two hot dogs with ketchup and a cherry soda. I certainly was glad when I felt my father's hand on my shoulder sometime later. I was just sitting on a bench, feeling queasy and getting all worried about everything. My head turned and I said, "How good was Citation?"

"Citation," he said and sat down next to me. "Don't worry about that shit right now. We're here, man. We're doing it." My father gestured in the direction of the tote board. "Bowl Game is just eleven to one. Did that myself, dropped him ten points." He laughed and then he was quiet again. You always wanted higher odds. Big bets at empty places like this always killed the chances of that. I wondered if he'd thought everything through. He rubbed his mouth and didn't say anything for a while.

Then the horses for our race appeared from the paddock tunnel. Bowl Game was number 2; his rider, Guillermo Milord, had an expression like someone standing near a headstone. My father stepped up on the bench, even though a sign attached to the hurricane fence down by the outside rail said *No Standing On Benches*. I did the same.

I had already seen hundreds of live horse races, but once this race started and the horses dashed by us the first time around, it was as if I couldn't hear a thing. I panicked, started to jump up and down. I said, "Go Bowl Game, come on Bowl Game! Go!" I could feel my heart throbbing and then, as the horses went around the turn I could hear the race caller's voice, which sounded far away. My father's arm was around my back and I just gyrated in place. Bowl Game was towards the back but it was going to work out. It felt possible. The field turned in to the stretch and the race caller didn't say Bowl Game's name. Whips popped, horses grunted. Bowl Game finished close to the inside rail, just one horse behind it at the wire.

The side of my father's face glistened. He dipped his head towards the pavement and was considering it as if it were a lot further down. He jumped from the bench. He turned, faced me and said, "Time." I let him stay a step ahead as we began walking for the parking lot. He walked fast, wanted to stay ahead.

I ducked into the Eldo and he backed up the car and then stopped it with a quick jerk. In drive again, the car sputtered but he kept on the gas and it shook some more, began to level out. "Unfortunate, this ride," he said. In a moment, we were moving under the towering palm trees. The Eldo ran choppily. When we finally pulled up to the Beau Rivage, my mother was already out there, sitting on the lowest step of the hotel entrance. She might've been worried, or she could've just heard the car coming up Collins Avenue. When she got in, she took the back seat and then she didn't say a word. No one did.

* * *

My father might've seen an advertisement for Lake Hiawatha on one of the billboards along the highway when we were past Fort Lauderdale, and the coughing of the Eldo must've already been on his mind. Sometime later, when we were at the lake, the three of us were post-losing-bet solemn. My father had edged the car to a section of grass. Before us lay a glassy blue lake. Without a word, he went to the trunk, opened it. My mother got out, went to the back of the car, and there they talked. He closed the trunk again and she helped him carry the bags over to a beat-up wooden picnic bench. My mother said my name and I got out of the car.

I wasn't sure what was happening until I was standing in front of my mother, the two of us near the picnic table, one hand of hers atop my head while my father stood next to the opened driver's door, the top half of him bent inside the car, the sunset beyond everything starting to turn peach and royal blue. He started the engine. He seemed to be fooling around in there. Then he brought himself out, glanced in our direction. I guessed my mother nodded. He ducked back in halfway again and she said, in a quiet manner, "All right, go ahead, do it."

Nothing had been said between them, but when my father jumped all the way into the car and then drove it right for the lake, my mother feebly said, "What?"

The Eldo didn't have much momentum when it reached the water, but it seemed to keep going anyway; tiny waves flickered at its sides and my father wasn't doing anything other than sitting behind the wheel. The Eldo seemed to catch some type of little swell, a crazy undertow, and it rose then and appeared to be rising, going faster. It floated to one side, began to take on water. My mother was already knee-deep into the lake by then. She dove and began to swim. I made it down to the water's edge, stood calf high, and by this time the car was up to its windows, my mother was breast-stroking for it. There was a wave near the driver's side at one point and for a moment there I couldn't see either of them.

I was up to my chest when they reappeared. They were like this odd, person-and-a-half creature, him at the waist of her jeans, hanging on. It was only when they were standing in the shallows again that my father turned. He looked at me, stuck his hands on his knees. The water ran off him like he was a fast-melting man. Once they'd trudged up to the shore, he moved over to a patch of tall grass and sat down in a heavy way. My mother stayed near the water's edge. An old man in gray pants and white t-shirt appeared, perhaps from the bait shop in the distance. Across the lake, a couple of people had been fishing and one of them was running back and forth along the shoreline.

My mother noticed I was watching something, and when she turned, the old bait-shop man was still about ten yards from her.

"Must have slipped into gear!" my mother said his direction. "We tried to stop it."

The man stopped, then he crossed his iguana-like arms. "Lady, you gotta get that thing outta my lake," he said, sort of twisting to one side.

She pushed back her hair with both hands and said, "Let me use your phone, OK?"

"What's going on here?" the man said. The car's roof was all you could see, a tiny island of glowing metal.

"What kind of fish do you have?" she said, as she slid her hands over her wet hair again.

"Bluegill!" the man said. "I saw you all taking the stuff out the car before it went into the lake!"

"Leave him be," my mother said because the old man's eyes were on my father. "He buried his parents today." Her voice was quiet at that. Then, she looked out to the lake, shaded her eyes.

When she turned again to the old man, she said, "Lemme use your phone, all right?"

My mother followed the man to the bait shack. My clothes clung to me. My father sat in the grass, looked out at the lake. I wiped under my nose with my index finger. My mother arrived at my side. "Cab's coming," she said. "When it arrives, get in, don't say a thing." She left me, stepped over in the direction of my father. She knelt near him, spoke, and he nodded. He smiled in the faintest of ways. The next time I looked over there, she had her hand near the side of his head, was tucking a sliver of his hair behind one ear.

The old man stayed away, kept close to the bait shop. And when the taxi appeared, it headed for us over the gravel road we had taken to get here. I waited for my parents to stand, and when they did and began to collect our cases, I started moving. The bait-store guy walked in our direction, but he didn't move fast.

After pulling himself into the front seat of the taxi, then taking a quick look to the back seat, to where my mother and I were, my father said, "Go!"

From the back seat, my mother held two soaked $20 bills at his shoulder. "My taxi cab is wet now," the driver said, with a big laugh.

"Hurry," she said.

"Yeah, we'll be back," my father said, calling to the old man, who'd stopped walking. The old guy looked out to the Eldo again. The cabbie, a Black man, had very dark skin, and he wore a straw hat missing its brim. We pulled out, traveled up the gravel road.

"Just drive for a few minutes," my mother said, in a clear way, from the back seat.

"Right," he said.

"Until I get this figured out," she said, then she turned and put her eyes on the passenger window.

* * *

One thing about my father's gambling trips was that someone always seemed to have some cash left afterward, money for a restaurant or a night out or, in this case, a motel, which was the Passport Inn, a $17 cab ride from Lake Hiawatha. I kept watching the meter, worrying about how we were going to pay for the next thing, and then I remembered I had something from the track, the money my father had given me. I reached into my pants pocket, held the clammy bills in the air. My mother nodded, then tapped my father's shoulder so he could see.

At another point, the cabbie did grin and say, "You went into the lake, yes?"

"Yes," my father said. "We're a family of swimmers. It's in our blood."

"The Passport Inn has a pool," the cabbie said, still smiling, his teeth bright.

The motel was just out in the middle of nowhere, all this Florida scrubland, and after the cabbie left us off, all I could see in the distance was an illuminated Orbit Truck Stop sign above the silhouette of a treeline. My father's clothes were still soaked when he walked inside to see about a room, and I would like to have heard the explanation he gave the clerk about that. I watched him intently from where I stood and, from behind, my mother's voice said, "Are you all right?" At that, I turned pretty quick. The damp fabric shrank to the shape of her shoulders and inside her shirt was the outline of her brassiere. She looked powerful to me. I might've appeared transfixed by her, so I looked away again. "He'd never driven in a lake before, that's what he said afterward. He said, 'Why waste the final ride?'" Inside the office, behind the glass, my father's shirt clung to him and for a second I wondered what it would've felt like, riding in the water like that. I understood that the car had been unlucky and it had to go. "He just doesn't plan ahead," she said, though her tone was not accusatory. It didn't seem like much of a sin to me.

When my father stepped outside again, he sniffed the sleeve of his shirt and this made me sniff my own. He had two room keys, and he handed one over to me and then started to pick up our bags. He said, "I think I'm going to change clothes and walk up there and arrange for the evening's supplies." No one said anything else. We walked past the filmy surface of the pool to a line of rooms with prefabricated siding, weak-looking pine doors. I had a room to myself and I had to open the window because it was like my school cafeteria in there—way too warm, like somebody was stewing meat. When there was a knock on my wall, I pulled my door back and went right over to their room. I guessed I still appeared a bit shook up because when my father answered their door, his smile shrank. "Hey, it's all right," he said. He reached forward, jiggled my shoulder. "Come on over here." The spread from the truck stop was on the bed: wrapped sandwiches, little bags of potato chips, a six-pack of beer, a carton of lemonade, two pints of vodka, two wrapped cupcakes. My mother had showered; her hair was wet, she was in different clothes. We sat around the food, on the bed, and their TV was on, the sound down to almost nothing. My mother said at one point, "Please go change."

"Let him eat," my father said. And I did. I started to feel better, and I must've been eating a lot because my mother gave me half of her ham-and-cheese and in no time just the cupcakes were left and my father scooted the plastic wrapper to me. He said, "Do you know how many racetracks there are?" My mother and I didn't say a thing. "Two hundred and nineteen," he said. "I won't see them all in my lifetime."

"No one wants to see them all," she said. "That's not a real ambition."

I thought maybe my father would start up with one of his talks, a future plan. He raised the back of his hand to his nose and sniffed. He seemed to be thinking about something. I couldn't smell anything, even though I was the one sitting there in the wet clothes. He said, “I didn’t say it was.”

“You’ve seen enough of them,” she said, in my direction. This startled me, and I felt like saying something back to her. If I’d been sitting in something other than my lake-water clothes, I might’ve. “The evidence is all on my side right now,” she said, even though I had kept quiet. “Don’t ever forget what you feel like right this minute.”

“I won’t,” I said. I knew better than to argue. The time to do that was before you went to the races. That was when there were still possibilities. Afterward, you just agreed on what you could. Two hundred and nineteen? No one could get to them all. Wasn’t how many the real question? Or where the next one would be? Those were the things you could start talking about, though not on days like this one. I guessed to her I might’ve just looked like a wet, hungry kid who didn’t know a thing. That was okay, I could be that kid, too. I’d be any kid they wanted, so long as they kept taking me along.

Mississippi

When she heard that her niece Samantha was moving back to Vicksburg, Morgan's first thought was that she ought to prevent it. Samantha's adult life had featured one misstep after the next, and that's what happened to people who kept screwing up out in the world: they finally gave up, went home. Morgan felt she needed to step in and do something. But the thing was, no one was asking for her help.

When she and Samantha were growing up, they saw how everyone's lives played out. Adults were defenseless and dispirited; curiosity about the world outside Mississippi seemed nonexistent. This was especially true of the people in their own family. They'd taken their chances, gotten away for a time. But they just couldn't handle it. They came back to Vicksburg, defeated forever. Morgan was nearly six years older than Samantha, so as a teen she was better able to see the traps. She vowed it would never happen to them. Morgan remembered their talks, their pledges, how young they'd once been.

Morgan had left home for college, attended Southern Miss down in Hattiesburg. She met the man she would marry and graduated on time. She and her husband moved to Atlanta, where they'd lived for the past twenty-nine years. They had one child, a son, who'd recently graduated from Georgia Tech and was spending part of the summer abroad. Samantha, like Morgan, had gone to Southern Miss after graduating high school. She wanted to take art classes. She dropped out during the fall term of her sophomore year, moved to Pearl River, got married, then divorced. She moved to New Orleans, got married there, then divorced. Then she moved to Baton Rouge, where she got married once again. Her third husband ran off to New Mexico with another woman; Samantha had remained in Baton Rouge. She lived in a series of crappy one-bedroom apartments, worked at low-paying jobs. She got tattoos, suffered from piercing migraine headaches. She always kept animals, mainly cats.

Samantha was forty-five now; they stayed in touch mainly via Facebook. They sent private messages to one another, and Morgan felt they still had a unique connection. But Morgan's older sister Sarah, Samantha's mother, was the one who informed Morgan about Samantha's plans to move back home. When Morgan decided to email Samantha, she wrote,

Hey Sami

What's this I hear about you moving back home. Anything I can do? Let me know.

Love, M.

Sarah was fourteen years older than Morgan; they had the same mother but different fathers. When she was younger, Sarah too couldn't wait to get out of Vicksburg. She skipped college and moved to Houston with a friend from high school. Sarah worked at a nightclub there, served drinks, met a man who got her pregnant. She had an abortion, then spiraled a bit. She ran up credit card bills, was arrested once for possession of marijuana. When she moved back home, she was broke and combative. While all of nineteen, she married a sheriff's deputy and had just turned twenty when she gave birth to Samantha. Not long after this, Sarah's husband got kicked off the force after being caught in a sting at a local motel. He'd been dressed in stockings and a peroxide wig. Looking for a fresh start himself, he moved away from Vicksburg. When Samantha was in grade school, the family received word that her father had been killed in a head-on car crash in Bowling Green, Kentucky. Sarah hadn't married again, though for a while she'd semi-seriously dated a libertarian from across the river in

Mound, Louisiana. They'd listened to conservative talk radio together.

After Morgan emailed Samantha, Samantha didn't get back to her for a couple of days. When she did, she wrote,

Hi Morgan,

Yeah, it's true. Sick of Red Stick. Out of options, as busted as an old banjo. Me and Mighty and Bella are heading up to the Vick. Going to stay with mom. (God help.) Haven't thought about anything past that. Worried about Mighty a little. She's asthmatic. Mom still smokes like a power plant.

Love, Sami

Sarah and Samantha would be aware of the fact that they didn't get along. Sarah's marriage to the deputy had been rocky from the start, and her mother (also Morgan's) was extremely critical of all the choices Sarah made. As a result, by the time Samantha became a teenager, Sarah was following in her own mother's footsteps, over-mothering her daughter. Samantha felt that Sarah had become a controlling, suspicious person, and when she'd gone away to college, those issues hadn't been resolved. Subsequently, choices made by Samantha were subject to sharp criticism from Sarah. This was not lost on Morgan, who sometimes was put in the middle of their arguments, even though she'd left Mississippi years earlier. That was especially true when Sarah dated the libertarian from Mound and frequently quoted conservative talking points. Samantha felt that her mother was losing her mind. After Sarah and the libertarian split, her views shifted again to the left. She identified herself as a Blue Dog Democrat. She and Samantha found other things to argue about.

Sarah's smoking would contribute to Samantha's headaches. Sarah, now in her mid-sixties, had retired from her government job and spent most of her days at home. The pension she received was modest, not enough to do much traveling on, not that Sarah was a traveler anyway. So, until Samantha got a job—and though Morgan was guessing here, she felt Samantha wouldn't be in any hurry to flip hamburgers or waitress for mouse-food pay—Sarah and Samantha would be stuck together inside that house for lengthy periods of time.

The night before Samantha was scheduled to leave Baton Rouge for Vicksburg, Morgan and her husband were out on the balcony of their Atlanta condo, which looked down to Piedmont Avenue and beyond that an entrance to Piedmont Park. Morgan kept her husband apprised of things happening with her family on a what-she-wanted-him-to-know basis. They sat on forest-green balcony chairs from Pier One. It was twilight, and the glow from the streetlights yellowed the leaves on the maple trees across the street. There were glasses of white wine on the table for two between them. She said, Do things always have to turn out badly?

Her husband, who knew Morgan's family just the same, said, I don't know. I mean, I do know, but you already know that. Why, I mean.

Why? she said. Say it.

Because that's the way it goes.

Well, I'm going to do something. I might walk back inside in a minute and call Sami directly, tell her I'm sending her ten thousand dollars. Give her the chance to find some other options.

Morgan felt her husband would step in here, caution her about "giving away" money. She frequently sent fifty- or hundred-dollar donations to do-gooder organizations. Especially if an injured animal needed an operation. Morgan's argument was that they had plenty.

He said, Same Samantha, same mistakes. Money won't change it.

Well, I can't dispute that, she said. But I'm not going to just sit here and say, Oh well.

Honey, it's been a long day, he said.

I'm going inside now, she said.

Upstairs, her small office was adjacent to their bedroom. Her husband hadn't done anything specifically to anger her, but occasionally his matter-of-factness about things was soul-crushing. She closed her office door, opened her laptop, checked her email and Facebook accounts. No second thoughts from Samantha, no twenty-third-hour change of plans. No one had asked for any help—Morgan reminded herself of this. It was Samantha's life. Somewhere down the road when regret filled Sami about moving back to Vicksburg, Morgan would listen. If and when Samantha wanted to bolt, Morgan would provide the funding.

Morgan could call Samantha right now, but it wouldn't be right. Samantha had so much on her plate. Getting her own stuff packed into her car, leaving a clean apartment behind her, situating her cats, including the one that had asthma. Samantha was already a depressed woman. They all were depressed in her family, every last one of them. When she'd been younger and raising her son, Morgan sought therapy. She felt so uncertain about how to raise a child. Over time, she grew stronger and more confident about this. Eventually, her therapist suggested they suspend her medication. Morgan handled that. She began to think differently about her depression. She told her therapist she wanted to take some time off from their sessions. She'd never wanted to be all squeaky clean and happy, she'd never hoped or asked for anything like that. She worried about erasing who she was. Every year now, she sent her therapist a Christmas card.

She sat in her office and thought about her therapist, maybe giving her a call, even though it was late for that. And they hadn't been keeping up with one another. The thing was that even though she felt anxious, it didn't seem unreasonable. Living with her mother again, Samantha would get even more discouraged; she'd sink like a stone. But what could Morgan do about that? Who knew, maybe Sarah and Samantha would get along...after all this time. But they wouldn't. There wasn't a thing Morgan could do about that. She wanted to intercede. But she didn't know how.

* * *

The following evening, Morgan checked Samantha's Facebook page and found a couple of new entries. Samantha reported that the drive to Vicksburg had been easy enough. She'd decided not to keep the cats in a carrier. Bella and Mighty had primarily stayed in the passenger seat, they liked the air conditioning. At the end of the day, Samantha was back in her old bedroom in her mother's house and the two cats were with her. The long ride and the smoky house did make Samantha queasy. The cats, too, she reported.

This was when Morgan had her idea.

Three days later, Morgan received an email from Sarah:

Hey Sis,

Hope you're okay. What're these huge boxes about? They have my name, I almost didn't take delivery, thought it was a mistake. Your name is listed as sender. What's happening?

Sarah

Morgan wrote back,

S,

Wanted it to be a surprise! All that stuff is for a screened-in room for your patio. For Sam's cats. I know she can't just let them roam. One has asthma. I'm going to fly over to Jackson, rent a car, and drive over to see you guys. Help you build it. What do you think?

Love, M

Later that evening, Morgan found a reply from Sarah:

M,

Okay. I guess we'll see you then. If it means that much to you.

Love, Sarah

The next morning, before leaving for their jobs, Morgan and her husband had coffee. She informed him of her plans. She knew he wouldn't object much. She said, This way, the cats will have a place to go to get out of the smoke. Samantha can, too, actually. It's a little thing, it's not a big deal. What will you do without me?

She was pleased, and a little anxious, and he could probably see that.

Not much, he said. Read headlines, find something to get angry about. Run in the park. Watch baseball. Want me to come with you, help build the…? I can get a couple of days off.

No, she said. Stay here. We can manage. When's Ben getting home from London?

Not until next week. You know, that's a pretty good idea. That house of hers is smoky as hell…went there after your mother's funeral. I could barely breathe.

It's her house, though. We'll see how it goes.

He eyed Morgan. That's pretty good, he said. I see what you're doing.

I think it'll help the cats, she said.

On Friday, her Delta flight from Hartsfield-Jackson left on time. She picked up her rental car at Medgar Evers International in Jackson and headed west on I-20. In her rolling suitcase, she'd packed her clothes, toiletries, gloves, visor, sunscreen. Sarah had emailed her the day before, said they could borrow whatever tools they needed from her neighbor, Bill Todd. Morgan grew anxious as she neared Vicksburg; she hadn't seen Sarah or Samantha in years. She went through a mental checklist of things not to talk about…one thing for sure: she didn't want to ask about anyone's plans. She drove west on the interstate; she recognized the names of the small towns she passed, and she turned calmer. Of course, if Samantha brought up something about the future, Morgan would listen, maybe offer an opinion. If Sarah wasn't around.

When Morgan pulled into the driveway of Sarah's ranch-style house on Boy Scout Road, both Sarah and Samantha stepped out from the front door. They wandered over to the car as Morgan dropped lip balm and breath mints into her purse. Once she was out of the car, Morgan lightly embraced Samantha, who'd come closer than Sarah. Look at you, Sarah said.

Morgan didn't want to seem self-conscious, so she didn't ask what Sarah was referring to in particular. They'd all gotten a little older. Morgan went over and put an arm around her sister. Sarah had gained weight, her always-thin hair had gone white. Samantha looked pale and her expression seemed distant. She had her tattoos; Morgan noticed the light-blue rose inside her left thigh. Morgan had her hands on her hips when she said, Let's go see about those boxes. Around back, Sarah had a patio with sliding glass doors that opened into the living room. The boxes were stacked on the patio, a half dozen of them, the one holding the aluminum beams ten feet in length.

Morgan noticed a black tuxedo cat sitting just inside the sliding door. That's Bella, Samantha said.

Is that the one with asthma? Morgan said.

No, that's Mighty.

She sleeps on the couch all day, Sarah said. Well, I've looked over all the directions. I borrowed all the tools we need from Bill. When do you want to start putting it together?

Morgan caught Sarah glancing in Samantha's direction. Morgan said, I'm ready to get going right now.

Let's do it then, Samantha said.

When they started, it was early afternoon, not a cloud in the sky. They removed all the pieces from the boxes and then they broke down the boxes and stacked them in the yard. Sarah said she would take them to the recycling bins at the County Market. She suggested how the order of things might be put together. She brought out iced tea. She volunteered to make a run to McDonald's. While she was gone, Morgan and Samantha continued to work. Morgan held two beams in place and Samantha used the drill.

After Sarah returned, the three of them sat in the yard and had hamburgers, fries, and Cokes. They talked about animals, the stray dogs in the neighborhood, the latest sightings of racoons and possums. Their mother's old friend Maylynn Bell kept so many cats that somebody had called animal control on her last month. Maylynn had a fit and animal control decided to leave it alone. The cats are probably better off with her, Sarah said. She does love them so.

They agreed they needed to get back to the screened-in room in a few minutes. They could go at it for a couple more hours. Tomorrow, Morgan would get there by nine and they'd work all day, try to finish everything. Sunday could be for trouble-shooting; Monday morning, Morgan had to get back to Atlanta.

They worked until after five. Then Morgan was saying to them, Hell, you guys, I'm beat. Let's call it a day.

Where you stayin'? Sarah said.

America's Best Value. On Frontage Road?

Sarah said, I think that's on Warrenton Road. You know where I mean?

Yeah, yeah. Website said they had a swimming pool that stayed open till ten. You guys want to check it out?

Maybe tomorrow, Samantha said.

I'll bring breakfast, Morgan said. See y'all in the morning.

While in Jackson earlier, she'd stopped at the Whole Foods and purchased two bottles of wine as well as a box of crackers and a bag of almonds. That evening, Morgan sat up in her motel room, watching cable TV, one episode of *Modern Family* after the next, and the episodes amused her. Her husband called, said he was sitting up in bed, reading Orwell's *Down and Out in Paris and London.* I'm worried we raised Ben too soft, he said. I grew up with nothing, you grew up with next to nothing, I've been thinking about it. Everything will crash, these goddamn Republicans… He's an only child, he's pretty spoiled.

We weren't going to ignore him, sweetheart.

We'll all be washing dishes for Putin soon enough, her husband said.

Honey, sounds like you had a long day.

When're you coming back?

Soon. Look, we raised him fine, she said. I'll talk to you in the morning.

* * *

When Morgan awakened, she could see the sunlight beaming in from around the edges of the drawn curtains. The digital clock said 6:48; she hadn't overslept. In fact, she had an extra hour because of central time. She lay in bed, felt stiffness in her arms and shoulders. There was the hangover from the wine. Her thoughts went to the call last night from her husband. If he was concerned, then all right, they could have a talk about that, but the talk would have more to do with her husband's outlook than what was happening with Ben, who was traveling this summer with his girlfriend, Julia. Ben was a terrific son, and they'd done their best with him. They'd raised him in a two-story house in Decatur; Morgan's husband was a regional executive for Marriott, she worked in HR at Emory. They had money, they didn't want for anything. After Ben left the house for college, they sold the house, made a nice profit, and moved to Midtown. They'd always be there to support him in any way they could. They would worry about him, there was no way around that. He was a college graduate. It was his life; he was on his own path. Her husband was aware of all of this.

When Morgan arrived at Sarah's house, she brought a variety of Ward's biscuits: butter, catfish, sausage link. Sarah and Samantha were already in the backyard, each of them in cut-off shorts, t-shirts, and baseball caps. Samantha had the blue rose tattoo inside one thigh; she also had a sword on one forearm, a broken heart on the other. Morgan noticed how handy Sarah and Samantha seemed to be, no doubt the result of living years without men. She let them have first picks with the biscuits; she wound up with the link, and it helped with her hangover. They worked as a team all morning, focused on the order of how things needed to be done. Bella, the non-asthmatic cat, stood at the glass door and watched them.

By early afternoon, they were hungry and needed a break. The construction of the screen room was going well. It would serve a purpose. A Chick-fil-A restaurant had just opened down on Clay Street, but Samantha said she wouldn't eat a crumb from a chain that didn't believe in LGBT rights. Sarah, who'd yet to try it, said that it was impossible to know the politics of every restaurant owner so why should that be in play now? Morgan agreed with Sarah's logic but said, Come on, let's choose another place. They agreed on Sonic because it was the closest. It was Samantha's turn to pick up food, and she said she was happy to go but she didn't have any money. Here, here, Morgan said, pressing a twenty in her hand. I want a chili dog and tots. Me, too, Sarah said. After they heard the car door close and a car engine start, Sarah and Morgan were looking at one another. She's broke, Sarah said. Got nothing.

Morgan felt something rising in her and was on the verge of saying *All she has to do is ask me for money, I'll give her whatever she needs.* But Morgan knew this wasn't the problem. She said, That'll wear on anybody.

She'll be all right, Sarah said. She knows she needs to get a job soon. She's not lazy.

Morgan said, No, she's not. I'm gonna step inside for a sec.

Yesterday, Morgan had been inside Sarah's house a couple of times, to get a glass of water, use the toilet. It was a smoker's house, there was no avoiding that. Morgan hadn't done much in the way of looking around. She wanted to stay working with Samantha and Sarah on the screened-in room. Today, she lingered. She stood at the window that looked out to Boy Scout Road; from here, she couldn't see the house she'd grown up in, but it wasn't far away. Like this one, a small, ranch-style house. She thought of her first bicycle, her friend Jenny Grant, whose bike had tiger stripes. Right after high school graduation, Jenny was killed in a car accident on Highway 49. Morgan thought of that tiger-striped bike; Jenny had always been so good about letting her use it. Seventeen years old, she thought.

She took a glass from the cupboard, filled it, walked out to the living room. She looked for anything different from the day of their mother's funeral, six years ago now. Worn-out brown sofa, knock-off brand flat-screen. Self-help books on the coffee table—as with libertarianism, a one-time fad. Maybe Samantha was interested in these books, or maybe Sarah just wanted her to be. Morgan went looking for the asthmatic cat Mighty, who it turned out was sleeping on Samantha's bed. As soon as Morgan sat on the corner of the bed, Mighty jumped down and trotted off for another room. Outside, a car door closed.

Morgan slid back the patio door holding the glass of water. By now, the aluminum beams were all in place. Out in the yard was the assembled awning that needed to fit over the screen room. They still needed to tack up the screens. A couple more hours and they'd probably be done. They sat in the yard and had their meals from Sonic. Morgan reminded herself to hit the gym every day when she got back to Atlanta. Samantha asked about Ben, what he was up to, and Morgan said he was traveling in England with his girlfriend and still thinking about his future. He's on his own, Morgan said. We're really proud of him. She cleared her throat after saying this. After she swallowed a tot, she noticed Samantha and Sarah watching her. Morgan shrugged. Okay, I admit it, she said. It's hard to let go.

Samantha pushed back the wrapper on her hot dog to get another bite, and while chewing she said, Hey, y'all, I hear it's gonna rain tomorrow. That's what the radio said.

Probably need to try and get this done today...if we can, Sarah said.

They finished their lunches, pulled on their gloves and worked together. Cloud cover, the first in two days, came around five and a mild breeze followed. By evening, they were finished. The screens had been installed, the door hung. The slanted awning fit perfectly. They were beat. Morgan said she was going back to her room to take a shower. Sarah suggested, as tomorrow was Sunday, they all ought to sleep in a little. Morgan didn't have to come by until noon. She gave them each a hug; she got into her rental car and drove back to her motel. She texted her husband:

Everything's going good. I'm exhausted.
Let's talk in the morning.
Love.

In the morning, she could smell the white wine in the plastic cup on the nightstand. A dingy-gray light came in through the slightly drawn-back curtain. After her shower, she could hear it raining. She didn't need to be over to Sarah's for a couple of hours at least, and she sat on the edge of the bed with the towel wrapped around her. The roof of the screened room would get tested. She didn't feel the way she had felt when she'd first heard that Samantha was moving back to Vicksburg, so perhaps something had been accomplished. She opened the towel and looked down the front of her. So, she was in her fifties now. She sighed and wrapped the towel around her again.

The three of them spent the early afternoon in the screened-in room, sitting on chairs Sarah had brought out from her dining room. Bella, the non-asthmatic cat, twirled around Morgan's ankles, then jumped onto Samantha's lap. Morgan caught aromas of bacon and burned toast. They watched for leaks in the new roof. They talked about local politics. Sarah caught Morgan up on people she might remember. Morgan talked about her job, the things she and her husband did on weekends. She said, I guess it's pretty much what you'd expect. She watched the rain falling on the road that ran in front of Sarah's house.

You know, she said, this little room is pretty good.

Shoulda had it done years ago, Sarah said. Very good. Thank you.

Morgan said, Always takes somebody else to see what's obvious. She froze for a second, felt she might've crossed a line.

Well, you are right about that, Sarah said.

Yeah, Morgan said, her voice quieter.

Sarah said, So, what're you two gonna do tonight?

Morgan glanced to Samantha, who was scratching Bella between the ears. Morgan said, You feel like doin' something? You want to go to the casinos? Dixie Belle?

I don't know about that, Samantha said. Supposed to stop raining soon.

I'm no gambler, Morgan said. So, you just wanna come over to the hotel? Bring your bathing suit? What about you, sis?

I'm too fluffy to get into any bathing suit, Sarah said. No thanks. I have some stuff to do here, take these tools back to Bill Todd. What time're you leaving in the morning?

Early. When I get back to Atlanta, I might try to do a half-day at work. If I want to. They owe me like a thousand vacation days already.

Later that afternoon, while the rain fell lightly, Sarah gave Morgan a hug while they stood near the driver's door of the rental car. Sarah said, Safe travels, kid.

Morgan drove for her motel, almost didn't need the wipers. She'd be happy to spend more time with Samantha, though for a minute she worried that Samantha would be coming over out of some obligation. What did they have in common anymore? Morgan tried to imagine how the world looked and felt to Samantha these days. What did she look forward to? What did she believe in? What reason did she have to get up in the morning? If Samantha did want to have a serious talk—something about the future and how it ought to be approached—Morgan would listen. Morgan wouldn't go on about her own choices. They'd been intelligent, obvious choices, and they'd taken her away from Vicksburg. Samantha had just returned.

Over the years, she'd imagined Samantha's life: late-night shouting matches with a husband she loved but who didn't love her...or maybe it was the other way. Worries about money, working at a job she couldn't stand. TV, lots and lots of TV. Hellish hot days. When Morgan arrived in her motel room, she drank the remainder of the white wine, then placed the empty bottle in a drawer of the bureau. She stretched out on the bed and waited for Samantha to arrive. She couldn't hear any rain.

Samantha and Sarah seemed so agreeable; maybe their relationship had changed over the years. Morgan knew that it probably had more to do with her coming over here and them working on the screened-in room together. The directions had been right there in front of them.

A text from Samantha:

parked outside, next to your rental

Morgan opened the door to her room just as Samantha was shutting the door of her Honda. The air felt warm and heavy and she had a shopping bag slung over a shoulder. In the bathroom of Morgan's room, Samantha changed into her swimsuit, a bright blue one-piece. Morgan stayed in her khaki shorts and loose-fitting t-shirt. The rooms of the motel were laid out in a square-C shape; the rectangular swimming pool seemed to be the gem of the property. Morgan claimed a lounge, watched Samantha breaststroke out to the deep end. Then she lay back, closed her eyes, wound up thinking about the above-ground pool Junior Lowry's parents had in their tiny backyard. His father, who worked in sales, had been promoted. When her eyes opened, a dripping Samantha padded in her direction. Morgan held up a towel she'd brought from the room.

Samantha sat on a lounge next to Morgan's and wiped at her face and shoulders. Whatever happened to Junior Lowry? Morgan said.

Who?

His folks had that above-ground...

Ah...kinda don't remember. Don't know.

You get to swim much?

Last guy I dated liked to go to the Gulf. Man, that water feels weird, though. All those oil spills out there.

Twilight approached; a streetlight beyond the rooms provided for a pyramid of gray light that fell all the way to the street. Samantha said, You swim, don't you?

I don't have your body; I'm not getting into any bathing suit.

Whatever.

I hope I haven't been too much of a pain for you guys. I just wanted to do something.

Samantha said, We're all shit and we don't deserve anything. You've got it nice and you feel guilty.

Morgan opened her mouth. She wanted to protest. There'd been all this politeness and tiptoeing about. Samantha said, Mom and I were talkin' about it before you got here.

Morgan shaded her eyes. Well, that could be true I suppose, she said.

You know, bad happens to me, good happens to you, Samantha said.

You don't believe in yourself.

No, I don't. Not lately.

When Morgan spoke again, she said, I don't why I should feel guilty. Though I'm not saying I don't.

If you weren't from here, you probably wouldn't.

Morgan said, I guess you've been reading those self-help books. She felt snarky, regretted it. She put her hand out, in Samantha's direction.

It's all right, Samantha said. Mom tries. I don't think she shoulda retired, though. All this time by herself.

She's probably glad to have you around.

It'll be that way for a little bit. Hey, I'm hungry.

Me, too, Morgan said, even though she hadn't been thinking about it.

Lemme me do a few more laps and we'll go out.

I'll wait right here for you.

Morgan closed her eyes and listened to the sounds of Samantha doing laps. The pool water must've felt really good to her. Then, at one point, Samantha was speaking, though it wasn't to her. A couple happened by, a man and woman in straw hats and boots. They'd stopped and asked her about the water. Samantha was right in the middle of the pool, her head above the surface. Don't think about how cold it is and you'll be fine, Samantha said. We'll keep it in mind, the woman said. Enjoy your swim.

* * *

Samantha showered while Morgan changed TV channels. Samantha emerged from the bathroom dressed, with her wet hair combed back. They agreed on a Cracker Barrel just down the highway. They ordered a bunch of sides: turnip greens, cornbread, mac-n-cheese, sweet potato casserole, and fried okra. They talked about Atlanta and Baton Rouge and agreed that the hot weather felt just as oppressive, but it seemed more ominous now. Samantha asked about all the places Ben had been to this summer. Morgan said, Dublin, Paris, Reims…his girlfriend is bright and very pretty. They'll probably come back and tell us they're engaged. He's still got a lot to figure out.

When the young waiter came by with the bill, she immediately held up her credit card.

In the parking lot of America's Best Value, Morgan and Samantha stood outside Samantha's Honda and chatted for another minute. Before Morgan knew it, they'd hugged again and then Samantha had gotten back in her car, driven away. In the bathroom, Morgan discovered Samantha had left the shopping bag with her swimsuit. But that was Samantha, always a little preoccupied, a little scattered.

The next morning, Morgan flew to Atlanta. She took the train to Midtown and walked with the suitcase rolling at her side for four blocks. It was just eleven in the morning, and she could've easily changed clothes and gone in to work. She decided against it. When her husband got home that evening, she kissed him and they sat down to the dinner she made, vegetarian chili. She told him the trip had gone all right; everyone was pleasant and worked together on the screened-in room. She told him they'd asked about him and Ben. Later that evening, they sat on the couch in their living room. He said, Did you go swimming? Is that your suit, on the shower rod?

Sami's, she said. She tried the motel pool. She forgot it. So I washed it for her. I'll be mailing it back tomorrow.

So she and Sarah are getting along? he said. That's pretty surprising.

It won't last, Morgan said.

In another moment, he said, No, I guess it won't.

In fact, it was a few days later when reports surfaced of issues between Sarah and Samantha. Samantha emailed Morgan and said Sarah was hassling her about getting a job. Sarah said if Samantha was going to stay in the house, she needed to bring in some money. Sarah was an early riser while Samantha liked to sleep in. Sarah didn't like tiptoeing around her own goddamn house. Then Sarah was writing Morgan about Samantha. She said the cats were on her kitchen counters. She said Samantha didn't like her cooking. Sarah wrote, I'm used to doing things my own way, this is my house. Morgan didn't take sides. Neither Samantha nor Sarah was asking her to do that, anyway. At times, she'd consider an email from Samantha or Sarah and forget about the screened-in room altogether. She still felt like it had been a good project, and she knew even though Samantha and Sarah were arguing again, they appreciated it.

A week after she'd come back from Vicksburg, Ben returned. Morgan and her husband drove down to Hartsfield-Jackson. They met the kids at the International Terminal; Ben hugged his mother and shook hands with his father. Julia gave them each a big hug. The kids looked tired and happy. On the drive back to the city, Morgan sat in the front seat, passenger side, while Ben and Julia were in the backseat, a rolling suitcase between them. The rest of the cases had somehow fit into the trunk. The conversation was pleasant, and at one point Morgan wanted to turn in their direction and say, When are y'all getting married? She was quite certain it would happen. It would be better to let them announce this, however. Their children would be glorious.

A week or so after this, on a workday before stepping into the shower, Morgan made a cup of coffee, sat down at the desk in her office, checked her Facebook page, her emails. She'd received one from Sarah:

Hey Morgan,

It's close to sunrise and I'm sitting out here on my screened-in patio, having a coffee and Camel Light. I get up early and I've started to come out here before dawn because I don't want to wake Sam. She's not a great sleeper, never has been. I have my laptop. This cat Bella likes it out here. It's quiet. I hear the crickets. I hear a freight train out there, heading west, I guess. I feel like time is standing still for a few minutes. I heard that same train when I was a girl if you know what I mean. I know you didn't build the room for me, because I didn't need it. But I'm glad to have it.

Love, Sarah

The email hit her. She'd felt something building for a while now. Morgan felt like crying, though Sarah hadn't written a note to make her cry. She'd just said thank you. Morgan couldn't help thinking of when she'd been younger and of all that she'd tried to avoid. She didn't have to turn out the way people in Vicksburg turned out, and it was this belief that carried her away from there. But right then, it felt like she would've been all right if she'd stayed.

She heard her husband's voice, calling from downstairs. She couldn't hear what he said, but she knew he was saying she was going to be late. She took a quick shower. She dressed for work, combed her wet hair. Downstairs, her husband was standing at the kitchen counter, phone to his ear. On hold, he said, in a whisper.

I gotta go, she said. She kissed his cheek.

Your hair, he said. He reached to touch it.

See you tonight, she said. Outside, as she headed up the sidewalk, she tucked a strand behind an ear. She thought of that above-ground pool at the Lowrys'. Junior's parents obsessed about the pool, wanted it sparkling, always overdid it with the chlorine. She could almost taste it now, after all these years.

Warehouse

You worked one summer at a warehouse across the street from Spring Grove Cemetery, in the third largest cemetery in America.

At lunch, you would sit with a couple of co-workers in an open loading bay and look out to the headstones and willow trees. The cemetery, known for its gothic monuments and natural beauty, was founded in the mid-nineteenth century. You told them what else you knew about it, that Union soldiers were buried there, along with other noteworthy people. When you said some of the names, your co-workers shrugged.

Any actors or ballplayers?

None that knew you of.

They liked to give you a hard time because you were a college boy.

For that summer, you didn't mind being one of them. You felt that work was important, no matter what type of work it was. You didn't want to be the type of person who seemed better off than a warehouse worker. You didn't talk about your plans for the future, which had nothing to do with working in a warehouse.

During your lunch break, you'd witness a man in a delivery driver's uniform and steel-toed boots jogging along the sidewalk outside the cemetery. The man, who had a squarish head and ash-colored hair, would jog to the end of Gerhardt Street, then make the left turn at Spring Grove Avenue and continue along the fences outside the cemetery. You would watch until he disappeared in the distance. He wouldn't come around again. One lap around that cemetery was a considerable workout.

You and your co-workers wondered about him; for example,

why didn't he wear running shoes? Sweat clothes? He, too, must've been on his lunch break, perhaps didn't have time to change. He was on the heavy side. Doctor's orders; better get in shape, or else. He probably worked at a warehouse nearby, had a dull, repetitious job. You and your co-workers agreed that jogging on the sidewalks outside a massive cemetery could at least help remind the guy that he was still alive.

You think of this now as you lean back on a bench in the city park, trying to catch your breath. You are fifty-six years old. You're wearing a jacket and tie, you're in street shoes. You wear a face mask. You just ran what must have been six city blocks. You weren't trying to catch a train or chase down someone who'd picked your wallet. You just started to run and…you ran.

You work from home these days, just a few blocks from here. You usually dress in jeans and a t-shirt; a polo shirt if you are Zooming. You don't wear shoes half the time. Today, you're dressed the way you are because you had a lunch meeting with a business associate. You met at a restaurant with outside, socially distanced seating. You had a productive discussion. Things were all right, business could be better, but it would look up, maybe after the election. It was the type of meeting you'd been used to, before the pandemic. It reminded you of the life you'd been leading, the way things had been going.

After lunch, you bumped elbows with your associate, then you each went in different directions. To start, you walked a half block at a leisurely pace. You started walking faster. Then, you were sprinting. You went against any number of *Don't Walk* lights. No brakes were slammed, no accidents occurred. Thankfully, traffic isn't what it used to be.

You sit on a bench in the park near the running track; you touch the cuff of your jacket to your brow. You try to calculate how many blocks you ran; there was Crescent to 13th to 12th to West Peachtree…did people notice? Of course they did, they had to. Maybe there was a policeman or woman who spotted you and wondered...but they wouldn't stop a man in a jacket and necktie who was doing nothing more than running as hard as he could. Not a White man, anyway.

You've adapted well enough to working from home. You and your wife have a townhouse; she works upstairs and you work downstairs. You do the work you did when you had an actual office to go to. Your work isn't as interesting as it was before. You've come to wonder about it, if it was ever interesting to begin with. You've told yourself that it will be good if and when the office is open again. But you've come to sort of hate the idea of this, too. You think about those quick affairs, to offset the stress, the tedium. Your wife had them, too. Who was she kidding?

Once the city went into shutdown, you and your wife agreed one benefit would be having more time together. Making-love wise, you joked that you'd need to try and pace yourselves. You've made love one time, in the spring.

From the bench where you sit, you can see people going at different speeds around the track. A couple in matching bright red tracksuits speed-walk together. A handful of young women in gold and blue outfits, probably from the track team at Tech, lope along, cover ground effortlessly. Inside the track are a couple of baseball diamonds. The sunlight falls across the diamonds and the track oval. It's approaching fall and there are touches of yellow and scarlet in the leaves of the trees.

You feel like talking, and it doesn't have to be with someone who knows you. Next thing, on your phone, you're looking up the number of Spring Grove Cemetery. Then, without any thought as to what you'll say, you're dialing. You raise the phone to your ear, remember to pull down your mask. The answer is automated, a male voice says, *Please select from the following four options:*

1-Funeral Home
2-Cemetery
3-Corporate Offices
0-Operator

You touch '2,' and on the second ring a person answers, a woman, older. "Oh, hello," you say. "I'm calling to…see…about maybe visiting. Anyone can do that, right? I used to work up there. I used to have a job in a warehouse."

"Yes, of course," she says. "Visiting hours are eight to six. Feel free to come and enjoy. We have literature at the office, you don't need an appointment."

"See, I wanted to be…," you say. "As far as literature goes, you mean?"

"Pricing plans."

"Oh, all right." You have a living will that states you'd prefer to be cremated, but you haven't stipulated yet where those ashes are to be spread. It's been hard to imagine a fitting place. Maybe you can ask her about it sometime, if this type of indecision is something that happens to a lot of people. For the moment, it seems too complicated of a subject. Her voice is kind. "Well thanks," you say. "Maybe I'll see you."

"We'll be here," she says.

You hang up, look out to the baseball diamonds; one is empty and at the other one, a man is underhand pitching batting practice with softballs. Four teens are spaced apart in the outfield.

She said, *Enjoy?* Well, it is a garden and a cemetery.

And what did you want the poor woman to say, anyway?

Your breathing has become steadier. You examine your shoes, see if they've been scuffed on the run. You settle back into the bench.

Your wife has a Zoom meeting this afternoon; she's told you when, but now you can't remember. If she's in the middle of something, she can just not take your call. She answers on the fourth ring. You say, "I didn't catch you, did I?"

"I came downstairs to get some lunch. What happened to that turkey and cheese sandwich we had in here?"

"That? I ate it last night. The bread was stale."

"Where are you, how was lunch with...uh?"

"Teddy."

"Teddy."

"Okay. I'm just sitting here on a bench in the park now. I need to get back, I know it."

"You can take an afternoon away."

You say, "Do you remember any of your summer jobs?"

"Sure," she says, after a pause.

"Tell me about one, real quick, just for the hell of it."

"Okay...all right." You understand that she is being patient. "I need to get out more, too."

"I'm watching softball practice."

"Cool," she says. "Yeah, I was a tour guide at one of the antebellum homes. I had to wear a dress with all these ruffles and lace gloves."

"I think you told me about that."

"It was either there or the Sonic, serving roadkill to Bubbas and sons of Bubbas. Being a tour guide paid better. I just did it the one summer. I felt like a goddamn fool."

"Let's do something tonight, sit up together and watch TV or something."

"Sure. That sounds good."

"You pick the show."

"Okay. You okay?"

"Yeah, I'm just thinking about things. We're still allowed to do that, aren't we?"

"I think so, sweetheart." Her voice is light. "Look, I'll see you when you get back here."

You slide the phone into the pocket of your jacket and look out to the diamond where the coach is pitching batting practice.

In a moment, you rise and walk in the direction of the field. You stand along the first base line, watch the coach underhand another softball in the direction of the batter. The coach wears a red ballcap, white baseball pants with black pinstripes, and a t-shirt with three-quarter-length yellow sleeves. Uniforms from different teams. His pulled-down mask rests at the base of his throat. He's a Black man who might be a few years older than you, and you nod when he glances in your direction. The kid at the plate has his mask down, too; he smacks line drives all over. "Drive it with your legs, that's right," the coach says. After a few more pitches, the coach turns to the outfield and waves in the left fielder. Another kid starts running in with his head down.

You say, "Hey, mind if I hit a couple?"

He is reluctant, you can see that. You're dressed the way you are. But maybe he understands enough. "Sure, Buddy. Go right ahead. Hang on there, Tony." The kid running in from the outfield winds up near third base.

You retrieve the aluminum bat lying next to home plate. You get into a batting stance. The coach lobs one in, you swing and miss. This happens again. He says, "Just make contact."

"Right," you say, in a murmur. You watch the next ball all the way in. You hit a slow roller to third base. The kid standing there bends down to scoop it up. The coach holds up an index finger and you nod. It's the same result, a grounder to third. You walk down the third base line, holding out the bat handle to the kid. You keep your distance. You give a wave to the coach. As you head in the direction of where you live, you give a final wave to the outfielders.

Later that night, you and your wife are situated on the couch, watching an episode of *Better Call Saul.* At one point, you reach over, take your wife's hand and kiss it. Credits roll. You agree to watch another episode. You think of those grounders you hit to third. What did you expect, when was the last time you'd even stepped into a batter's box? And on top of that, you were in street clothes. You remind yourself of that. You think of the park, the way the sunlight falls across the baseball fields on a late afternoon near the end of summer.

Room

Bill Curci's sales route spanned from Akron to Wheeling to Harrisburg. A town in West Virginia named Steelage had a motel, the Inn of Steelage, he grew to like because the motel proprietor, Maggie DiMaggio, would sleep with him when he stayed there. Right after the third time they were together, she explained that her husband, too, was frequently on the road. She usually didn't make love with the customers. She had chosen Bill, in part, because he showed up dressed in a jacket and a pressed shirt. "You arrive in the evening and you still look neat," she said. "It looks like there is something left in you. When you run a place like this, that matters." Maggie explained that in the future, when Bill came through town, it should always be on a Sunday evening. Her husband would've already left Steelage for southern Ohio.

She and Bill were in bed together, side by side.

"What does he sell?" Bill said.

"What?" she said.

He didn't answer.

"Sundays, okay?" she said. "But not a lot of them."

"All right," he said.

One Sunday afternoon, in the fall, he arrived at the Inn of Steelage, and after he tapped the bell on the counter twice with the tip of his index finger, a man stepped out from the doorway beyond the desk. The man touched a napkin to his mouth and then held it at his side. He said, "Need a place?"

Bill's eyes went to the doorway, which framed the pineapple-colored light coming from the room beyond it. Bill could smell fried chicken. His heart turned. He'd been married once. Arriving home in a jacket and tie was not enough, he remembered that. These days, it simply felt like what he was capable of. He'd been lucky to find a woman like Maggie.

"Room?" the man said, when Bill remained silent.

"A single, yes," Bill said.

The man guided an info card towards Bill, who stared at him a moment longer. "Got a credit card?" the man said. He had a boxer's nose, flattened, heavy-looking eyebrows and brush-strokes of gray at his temples.

"Your dinner is aromatic," Bill said. He thought that Maggie could hear and he didn't want to sound afraid. "I guess I'm hungry. Can you recommend anything?"

The man's fingertips were already pecking at the keyboard of the computer behind the counter. Then he said something that sounded like *V-8 Chapeau*.

"Excuse me?" Bill said.

"Vietnamese place," he said. "Take a right on Elm Street. They'll be open on Sunday, right?" He said this last part in a louder voice.

"They will," a woman's voice said from the lighted room.

The man said, "Tell them you're staying here, you'll get a ten percent discount. They can use the business."

Bill was given room 5. He opened the door, but then he suddenly couldn't bear the idea of this room without Maggie's arrival to look forward to. He decided to get back into his Acura. He was not in the mood for exotic food, but he invented the somewhat desperate idea that Maggie would show up at the Vietnamese place. She'd heard what her husband had to say.

The restaurant was in a small, detached, beige-painted building that stood on the same block as a tire repair shop. The words *Viet Chateau* were illuminated over the entrance in strawberry neon; inside, a slight, dapper man in a jacket, white shirt, and powder-blue necktie stood at a podium. Beyond him were tables covered in white tablecloths. At the center of each table, a slender glass vase held a single red rose. There were only two other people in the room, a couple dressed in overalls seated by the window that looked out over the vacant street.

"Anywhere you like," the maître d' said with a sweep of his arm. Bill selected a table for two near the back of the room. Inside the restaurant, music played what seemed to be a techno-dance version of "Slave to Love." The paper menu listed *Sea Bass* as *See Bass* and after reading this, Bill flipped the menu over a couple of times. The couple seated by the front windows had fried platters of something and they ate steadily.

The maître d' happened over. He smiled a piano-key smile, and Bill wanted to ask him what kind of deal he'd gotten on the caps. He had black hair and kind eyes and Bill supposed he was of Vietnamese descent. He'd had a vision for this restaurant, this man, and as he stood with his hands behind his back, Bill unexpectedly recalled an intermission of a hockey game he'd attended in Wheeling, where a long red carpet was rolled onto the ice and then, from a tunnel at the far end appeared a small woman sitting atop a unicycle. She steered the unicycle onto the carpet, and then she balanced herself without touching her feet to the pedals. She held out her right foot and an assistant stacked small bowls on the foot, right-side up then upside down, and then, when the unicyclist was ready, she kicked them high in the air and they somehow landed all sleeved together atop her head. She tilted herself forward on her unicycle and leaned back again. The tall stack of bowls weaved like a caterpillar. Bill remembered cheering. It all was just right; sometimes Bill felt this way, too.

"Quite a lovely place you have here," Bill said. "I'm not kidding."

"Thank you."

Bill said, "I'll have a double bourbon, please." He held over the menu. "And for dinner, whatever you recommend."

"Right away," the maître d' said.

"Oh, no hurry," Bill said, after he was gone.

When the bourbon arrived, Bill drank it down and ordered another. He had the special, which was a rice dish prepared with sweet shrimp and pork, and it was not until an hour after he'd returned to his motel room that he began to feel sick. He had to race for the bathroom and he stuck his head down in the toilet just as he lost control. Afterward, he sat on the floor with his back against the bathtub. He began to wait for the next jolt of nausea. When it hit, he ducked his head towards the toilet again. He wiped his mouth with the back of his hand and closed his eyes as he flushed it. Maggie was married, and he hadn't worked hard enough to have as much as he did with her. He would be punished, there was no escaping it. The world is despicable, he thought. There was never something for nothing, you always had to pay.

Bill continued to be sick. It went on. He tried to think of anything to make himself feel better. He tried to think of times when he had felt better. He tried to think of times when he'd felt worse. It was all quite unconvincing. It'll pass, he thought. Bill knew this much, but it was all he knew.

He felt steady enough to go to the bed. He lay down and closed his eyes and waited for the next moment he'd have to rush for the bathroom. He lay still for the longest time. When he heard the doorknob lock turn, something tightened inside his chest. The door was opened and then closed again quickly. "Hello?" he said.

Without a word, the person who entered walked over to the bed. Then, the person laid down next to him. "I have about five minutes," Maggie said.

"I ate something bad at the Chateau place," Bill said, in a whisper.

"You don't have to whisper," she said. He heard her sniff. "Yes, well, I guess you did."

Bill said, "I don't want you to see me like this."

"I can't see you very well," she said.

In a second, he said, "Maggie."

"Yes?"

"Well, maybe it's not such a great idea that we keep this up."

"Well, why?"

"That guy is your husband, right?"

"He was my husband the last time you were here, too."

"You know what I mean, Maggie. I've seen him now. Things don't feel as easy." Bill wanted to reach for her hand.

"I thought you might worry," she said. "My husband wanted to surprise me today, that's all. He made me dinner and everything."

"That's pretty good."

"Yes, it is."

"Don't you feel bad, Maggie?" he said.

"A plate of chicken wings doesn't change all that much."

Bill said, "I ate the special tonight."

"I wouldn't have recommended that restaurant necessarily," she said. "I heard Raymond tell you about it and I almost got up to offer another suggestion. But he knows the owner. They play cards at the VFW hall. Anyway, I thought if the three of us were in the room together, you'd feel threatened."

"What happened when you heard it was me?" he said. She didn't answer right away, and he said, "Maggie?"

"I'm thinking," she said.

"You aren't going to hurt my feelings."

She gave a little laugh.

"You're not," he said.

"I'm trying to say what I felt in an accurate way. I'm not in love with you, Bill, but you already know that. When I heard your voice, I wasn't too surprised. I knew everything would be okay. Because you and I aren't in love, are we? I'm on your route. You're my customer."

He thought about sitting alone at the restaurant earlier. "No," he said. "I suppose we aren't."

"While you were out there talking with Raymond, I thought what a shame this is. I have two men tonight. I will wake up one morning later this week and there won't be any." She said this in a light way. She seemed ready to give a soft laugh. He was ready to hear something like that. She said, "I want you to keep coming back. That's what I wanted to say."

Bill said, "Why?"

"Because of this," she said. She moved her hand back and forth in the air, he could make out the motion. "Just this, you know. Talk. Different kind of talk. It's nice. I'm not going to beg you to come back."

"You don't have to."

She reached over and squeezed his hand. Then, she was on her feet. She seemed to be looking down at him. "Can I bring you an antacid? Anything?"

"No," he said. "It'll pass."

"All right," she said. "And listen, you don't have to make the bed, OK? Last time, you did that. I was surprised by it."

"I was grateful," he said.

"I had to change the sheets," she said. "Anyway, don't make the bed. When I open the door, I want to see that someone was here. I am not ashamed. Do you understand?"

In a moment, he said, "I am here."

"That's right, Bill," she said. "Have a little faith."

"Good night, Maggie," he said. "I look forward to seeing you again."

"Good night."

When Bill opened his eyes in the morning, sunlight shone from behind the gauze-like, royal blue curtains. He thought the room still had an odor to it. Dressed in his clothes from the night before, he went out to his car and removed samples from the trunk. He went back to his room, his bathroom, and began to clean every inch of it. It wasn't as if he had vomited all over the place. When he finished cleaning the bathroom, he decided the window ledges could do with a wipe-down. The edges of the off-brand flat screen. That done, he stood by the door and studied the bed. He lay down on the side of the bed where she'd been the night before. He tried to think about what she might think about, though he found this impossible. He stood again, walked to the door, checked how the bed looked. There were the impressions of two people..

Bill returned his cleaning products to the trunk and removed the hanger holding his clothes for today—pressed jacket and trousers—from the hook inside a passenger-seat window. He showered, shaved, and dressed in an efficient manner and then stuffed his wrinkled clothes in the small laundry bag he always brought on the road with him. He sniffed the air inside the room, then walked out to his car and returned to the room with a small bottle of air freshener. He pulled the trigger twice, watched the mist disappear into the faint sunlight inside the room, sniffed again, then closed the door behind him. He stepped out into the broad sunlight of a Steelage, West Virginia, morning and there stood her husband up by the registration office, sweeping away the autumn leaves that had gathered on the ground outside the entrance.

Bill didn't want to be frightened but he also didn't want to seem cavalier. He stood by his Acura and Raymond continued his sweeping. Finally, Bill headed in his direction. Raymond looked up when Bill was just a couple of steps away. Bill held out the room key and said, "Here you go."

"Oh, all right," Raymond said. He accepted it, dropped the key into his shirt pocket. "Need a receipt?"

Bill thought for a moment, then he said, "Yes, I do."

"Follow me." He stayed a step ahead of Bill as they approached the registration office. Inside, Bill stood opposite the counter from him. "How was the food last night?" he said, after tapping a button on the keyboard. The printer hummed.

"It was sufficient."

His eyes went to Bill, then to the computer screen, then back to Bill again. "It says here you've stayed with us a few times already. Where do you normally eat?"

Bill said, "I usually don't. The road takes away my appetite." He bobbed on his heels. "But like I said, your food last night smelled good."

"Yeah, the road does that to me, too." His hands were on the counter and he watched Bill. "You know my wife then?"

Bill metronomed his index finger in front of him. "The lady…who works here?"

"Yeah, the lady who works here. You're a salesman, I guess. What do you sell?"

"Cleaning products."

"Why don't you try to sell us anything?"

Bill slid his hands into his pockets and said, "Your rooms are clean. This is a nice place you have here."

"We like it," he said. He watched Bill for another moment, then reached around to the printer. He pushed the receipt across the counter.

"Thanks," Bill said. He folded the paper, tucked it in his shirt pocket. "See you next time," he said.

"We'll be right here."

Bill turned, moved for the glass door. He put both hands on the chrome handle and pushed it open. Outside again, the last thing Maggie's husband had said still hung in his ears. Bill felt the morning sun on his back. So will I, he thought. In the distance, the hood of his Acura held a pair sword-blades made of white sunlight. He walked steadily in that direction.

PSH

I spotted PSH in the park close to where I live. He and I were the only people on the oval track, running the same distance around, though in opposite directions. I tried not to stare but I did, and he seemed to wince when we went by one another. Red ballcap, chestnut hair flapping. Freckles, earbuds, white t-shirt, Bermuda shorts. A burly but not ungraceful man. The next day I read in the local paper that he was in town to make a movie but soon would be headed back to New York. A week later, I read a story that said he was dead. I would read stories about his death, but in the end I decided it would be better not to believe them. Of course, I didn't look for him in the city park close to where I live in order to prove that the stories were inaccurate. But I felt someone would catch sight of him again in NYC. And, in the end, that sorrow would have been wasted.

I already owned a number of films he'd been in; after the news of his death, I watched the films and decided that in each of them he seems to be doing pretty well. His characters aren't without their troubles. But they also aren't without the blessings of humanity.

Someone had already given me a copy of a film, *Owning Mahowny*, because it's about gambling—more specifically, a compulsive gambler who winds up losing millions. It's a great story and sometimes it makes me think of when I was younger and what I'd dreamed of doing. The non-dead actor embodies the role of the helpless gambler and the character moves carefully through his life, which is precisely what a gambler must do in order to keep playing. Then, there are the binges. In one scene, he steps away from a late-night self-implosion at an Atlantic City casino. He takes a walk along the beach. He is, as always, dressed in a cheap suit. At one point, he stands close to the surf, and when a meek wave rolls up his feet, he takes a little kick at it. The untrue stories about the death of PSH cited drug addiction, and when I read them, I couldn't help but think about the little kick at the dark ocean. In the film, I can tell you that the gambler does return to the casino. After he's gone, the moonlight shimmers all over the dark water.

Fortune

Paula Ghattas and I were planted in traffic in a champagne-colored Acura, a rental. I had the wheel, so she began to fiddle with the radio. I said, "Okay, whatever the song, you have to get on your phone and find out something the artist has done that's notorious. And it can't have anything to do with how spoiled they are." She hit a station playing "Cleopatra" by The Lumineers. "Good luck," I said.

The streetlight posts were barber-poled in red-and-green tape; it was a week before Thanksgiving. The sky had darkened, a band of fuchsia hovered over the horizon. It made me think that somewhere out there was a massive, pulsating party. Paula rolled her fingertip across the screen of her phone. "Well, it looks like they hired their cello player by placing an ad on Craigslist. Craigslist is kinda scary."

"It turned out okay. I don't think that counts."

"Maybe that's what I shoulda been doing. Placing ads that state what I need specifically."

"I wish you well with that."

"I know what your ad would say. *I need a winner.*"

"Think of how inexpensive it would be to run it."

She laughed, said, "There's a plus." The racetrack where both Paula and I worked back in West Virginia, Steelage Park, was a month away from being shuttered forever. Earlier that afternoon, we'd flown from Huntington to Miami. After we picked up the rental car, our first stop was the races at Tropical Park. We'd lost a little money there. Now, we were driving for our motel. Our relationship was pretty much on the rocks. Paula already had a job lined up at a track in Cleveland.

The next song began, "Halls of Sarah" by Neko Case.

"This station is growing on me," she said.

"We are in paradise." I wouldn't be going to Cleveland with her. She'd thought things over and decided she wanted a fresh start in some categories. The trip to Miami had been my idea. I said we ought to prove a breakup didn't have to be full of accusations and regrets.

This was Hail Mary time for me. I thought I could do something to change her mind. And I thought that despite her plans, she wanted to give me the chance. We'd played light at Tropical, ten dollars a race, long shots. I tried not to be too impressed by the famous jockeys and the slick, athletic horses. It was a world away from the Rust Belt, and in a way, I guess this was one point I was trying to make to Paula. Anyway, I wasn't really into the betting part of it, not on this first day. Nothing hit for us. We weren't even close.

When I'd first learned about Steelage going down, my main thought had been, Okay, where to now? Hawthorne? Fort Erie? Mountaineer Park? I didn't panic. Paula made some calls for herself and discovered that an old buddy of hers, Stacey Furniss, who was working in the publicity office at Thistledown, was six months pregnant. Paula called Stacey and it turned out all of what Paula had been told was true. Stacey had some mild backaches, pretty intense nausea. She needed someone to fill in for her...and soon. Paula told me the two of them had once had a big fight over a guy when they were working on the backstretch at Garden State in Cherry Hill, New Jersey. Paula had chased Stacey with a pitchfork. Stacey was pregnant and happy now, and Paula said the subject never came up.

Paula had freckled skin, long black hair. A tall woman with her eyes a touch too close together. She had been married twice before. She laughed a little now and then she said, "All right, get this traffic moving, I'm ready to reach the beach." She leaned over and kissed me on the cheek.

"I printed out a map," I said. "Just reach into the back seat. Hand that case to me. Already Googled the directions, track to motel. Tomorrow's *Racing Form* is in there, too."

"The basics." Paula snapped open the case. It was something I'd owned for years. Once, I'd had a bright idea about going back to business school, got so fired up I went out and bought the briefcase. Paula poked around in there, then I could feel her eyes on me, on my profile.

She brought out the rubber-banded stack of hundred-dollar bills. "Your meth lab doing well?"

"That's my entire savings. Seven grand."

She held the money between her thumb and index finger. "And what're you telling me?"

"Tomorrow," I said. "One horse. I'm gonna do it all on one horse. I wanted to just get a feel for things today. I wasn't going to say anything."

"You weren't?"

I lifted both of my hands from the steering wheel. I wanted to smile. "You're leaving. Steelage is closing. I make a big bet like this on a horse back home, it'll kill the odds. This is the major leagues down here. Tomorrow's a Saturday, a big-handle day. If I find the right one, I can really do something. I win, I can stay all winter. You can live with me, rent-free. No work. Just...personal freedom."

"Terrific."

I didn't say anything.

"Henry, I know you. Goddamnit, after all this time, are you telling me you can't live without me?" She waved the money, then she tossed it back into the opened briefcase and latched the case shut. I watched her from the corner of my eye. "I won't let you do this." She unsnapped the case, took out the money again. She pulled away the rubber band and folded the bills, stuck them into the pocket of her jeans. "I'll give it back to you when we're in West Virginia."

Traffic loosened; she still hadn't read me any directions. A new song: "Forgotten Years" by Midnight Oil. I tried to think of things I knew about that band. Wasn't the lead singer, Peter Garrett, close to seven feet tall?

We eventually found our motel, the Conquistador. A bit run down visually, but right on the ocean. We checked in, took a walk out to the surf, removed our shoes, stood ankle-deep in the cold water for a few minutes and looked out to the navy-colored sky. I supposed she'd put the money back in the case; her pockets seemed flat, empty. After that, we walked back to the motel, our room, changed clothes and went to the Tony Roma's across the street, where we ate and drank too much and talked about racetrackers we knew.

Back in the room, we kicked off our shoes, switched on the cable TV. They were having a *Godfather* marathon on A & E and we tried to remember which of the trilogy had a scene at Hialeah, the great Miami track that only ran quarter horses now. "Al Pacino was in a white Rolls," she said. She seemed halfway asleep by then. "Tropical's not too bad, though, huh?"

"Where's my money?"

"Safe," she said. "Shh."

"Paula."

"One day, I want to live in Cuba...me and Andy Garcia. You'll see."

* * *

In the morning, I awakened to a warm to-go cup of coffee on my nightstand. I said Paula's name a couple of times, but she wasn't around. I took a sip, then yanked away the covers and began to search the room. She'd unpacked her clothes last night, set them in the pine bureau by the off-brand flat-screen. Not much, a couple of t-shirts, jeans, underwear. The small room made for a quick search, the money nowhere to be found. My briefcase sat right on the table for two under the one window in the room. Not in there.

When Paula returned, I was sitting up in bed, looking over the *Form.* She wore sneakers, khaki shorts, an orange-and-white-striped t-shirt. She closed the door, then leaned her back against it, like something outside was getting close. "I want to show you something. Get dressed," she said.

"Good morning," I said.

"Come on."

I laid the *Form* on my lap. "Where's the stash?"

She leaned her head back until it touched the door. "You want to fight with me on this trip...I want to explore."

"I don't want to fight."

"What's with the fucking money?"

"I actually see a horse I like today. Maybe a lot."

She had her hands behind her back, maybe both of them on the doorknob. "Henry, your savings is on its way home. I drove around this morning, got a cashier's check at the Sun Bank. Found an open post office. Decided to mail it certified back to the apartment in Steelage." Her eyebrows went up. "All right?"

"I need it now."

She reached into her pocket and then she held up a slip of paper. "The receipt from the post office." She tucked the paper into a pocket of my briefcase.

"You're not my wife," I said.

"No shit. And I'm not going to get dragged into something here. We were crazy trying this."

"So, I have nothing to bet?"

"I'm gonna be at the Jumping Java across the street. I'll wait for twenty minutes. If you're not there by then, I guess we have nothing else to talk about."

She closed the door behind her.

Back in Steelage, neither of us would've been acting this way. Our relationship had been low maintenance, we gave one another plenty of space. Earlier this spring, she began to see another man in town. A man who wore a sport jacket, a wine wholesaler. There were a couple of female grooms I knew who lived in the dormitories on the backstretch, and I went in that direction from time to time. Things turned too swampy, and we re-pledged fidelity. The announcement about Steelage closing came about a month after that. Anyway, I did want her to see the money, I couldn't possibly deny that now. I simply hadn't anticipated her doing what she'd done about it.

Less than twenty minutes later, I pulled open the glass entrance door to Jumping Java. Paula sat at a table for two in the middle of the place. This said to me she wanted me to find her and that she didn't want to argue. When I slid in across from her, she offered a quick half-smile. "It's fine, it's OK," I said. She regarded me in a patient way. My eyes went around the room and I said, "I can always come back here after Steelage closes."

"That's right," she said. "You can."

"I want to do something good today. I feel like it's possible."

"Have a coffee," she said.

The shop was crowded; couples, mothers with children. I said, "Look, is there something you wanted to show me? Did you mention that?"

"Mmm-hmm."

"Well, I'd like to see it. Whatever it is."

Paula's eyes went down to her mug of coffee. "I don't know, Henry. Things feel kind of tainted."

"Look, I just want to spend the day with you. I don't even have to go to the races."

"Maybe I want to go to the races. Have something pleasant to think about this winter."

"Sure," I said. Though it didn't come out strong.

She waited another minute. I didn't blame her. "It's back across the highway," she said. "We'll have to do some walking."

* * *

Paula said that we wouldn't need our shoes and we dropped them off at the room. Barefoot, we headed across the asphalt lot and out to the sand. The sky had turned a filmy, turquoise color. I felt tired and hungry right away, but I didn't want to say anything. I guessed that Paula couldn't be in the best of moods because she had little to say, and while we walked, which we did for ten minutes or even longer, I tried to imagine where she could be taking us. Maybe there was something left over from a shipwreck. Or the remains of an orca. The ocean looked calm, the waves rolled up to the shore, retreated, dissolved. I thought of trips I had taken to Atlantic City. I loved Atlantic City, but my times there never quite worked out like I'd envisioned. I usually had a woman with me, had talked her into believing all the luck in the world would be waiting for us. I'd taken a few solitary walks on the boardwalk. Same ocean, I thought now. Though Paula had certainly hung in there better than the others.

"There," she said. We came to a sign that said, *Beware, Bathers Ahead May Be Nude.* The letters on the sign were printed neatly on a plywood square nailed to a wooden post. In the distance ahead, I could see bathers, a few of them, standing in the surf. The air felt warm and hazy. I said, "Wow, I don't feel like taking off my clothes for anyone right now."

"Optional," she said. "Come on." She stepped around the sign, ahead of me. I went after her and then, side by side, we walked along. Right away, I tried to think of the last person—beyond Paula or any girlfriend—who had seen me nude. I guessed some doctor, though I couldn't remember the last time I'd had a physical, had someone medical update my overall condition. You didn't need to do all that when you applied for work at a racetrack. No degrees, no transcripts, no pissing in a jelly jar. You got the chance to work because you knew someone and the someone who knew understood how important it was for you to stay in the game. Before you were licensed, they ran your record, made sure nothing was outstanding. The important thing always was that you knew the life, and you knew better than to complain about anything.

Approaching were a couple of nude men, each with long gray hair and mustaches. They were talking to one another in Spanish, the shorter one gesturing with his hands. They walked on, didn't seem to notice we were there. The *Beware* sign was maybe a hundred yards behind us, and I wondered what happened if these nude guys went beyond it, and if the nudes here strayed often from their boundaries. The sand felt warm and heavy. Paula shielded her eyes with one hand and looked out to the glittering ocean. Three men with clay-colored skin stood in the shallow surf there. I guessed they'd been at this for a while. There were women around, too. Narrow, wide, beige, brown. No one seemed to be in a hurry. There wasn't a big nude kickball game going on or anything. I shaded my eyes and looked in the direction of the three men. They toked on dark cigarettes. They noticed we were watching, and a bald one waved in a guarded way. We continued walking and nudes continued to pop up around us. For a while, we were the only clothed people, but then a jogger in sneakers and sweats went by, an older woman who looked amused. We kept walking. "When does it end?" I said, in something just above a murmur.

"Soon," she said. I couldn't be sure what she was thinking about. I wondered if things could work out to my advantage after all. I was younger than many of the people on this beach. I had pretty thick hair on my chest, which I was suddenly glad about. I thought about taking off my shirt, though I decided against it. "Let's sit," she said. Of course, the nude beach could not last forever, and in the distance were volleyball nets where people played in bright-colored swimsuits. Paula and I took a few steps in the direction of the surf and then she lowered herself. She stretched out her legs, crossed them at the ankles. She tossed her head and looked out in the direction of the water.

Her arms looked really pale to me. The ocean had turned calm and flat, the sky blue and endless. Nudists were in our peripheral, to the left and to the right.

"Maybe we should've had children." She looked out to the water and said, "I'm going to have children one day."

I had my legs stretched out too. I looked at my toes. "I'm sure you will," I said.

She sniffed and said, "Didn't you think of having children with me?"

"Sure," I said.

"When did you ever think of that?"

"Sometimes right after…we made love."

"You're kidding."

"No." I brushed at a band of sand sticking to my thigh.

"I'm on the pill."

"I know that. After we were together, I'd lie back and my mind would drift. I'd think, Suppose that actually caught? I'd think of how you'd look when you were pregnant. It seemed sexy. I guess it was pretty exciting."

"Oh, foo," she said. She picked up a handful of sand and tossed it right on the area of my thigh I'd just made clean. Then she seemed to reconsider something and began to brush it away. I looked up and there were two men between us and the waves. One was bald on top, gray at the sides, no muscle tone, a pot belly. The other guy was burly, and he wore a gold chain around his neck and sandals on his feet. They each held a dark cigarette, the electric, smokeless kind. They moved closer, peered down at us. Paula had the back of her hand close to her face. She held her fingers apart so she could see.

"Hey, fellas," I said. I supposed we'd broken a nude beach rule. Have clothes, can't linger.

They nodded to us. The one with the chain said, "We were watching you. Becky, Becky Jumper, right?"

Paula still held up her hand. "What?"

"You're Becky Jumper," the man said. He motioned with his electric cigarette. Then he took a puff from it.

The other man smiled and nodded. "All right," he said.

"Her name is Paula," I said.

"No," the man in the necklace said. "You're Becky and you're from Quincy, Mass. I met you at a club like two years ago. In Boston. You signed a cocktail napkin for me. You remember," he said.

Paula's mouth had opened.

"That club, West Deck. The cast from your show was there. Me and some buddies were hanging out. We had drinks with all of you. You were really fun, man. Except for a couple of the guys. They were, like, total morons."

"Right," the other said.

"What show was this?" I said.

"That thing on MTV," the guy with the necklace said. "You know, the thing where they crashed all the stuff."

I said to Paula, "When were you going to tell me?"

Both of the men standing over us laughed. "Get a load of this guy," one said. "This is like Becky Jumper here, man."

She had lowered her hand by this point. She peered up at him. "And here you are."

Each took another draw from his electric cigarette. The necklace guy said, "So, what's going on? What are you doing later?" The man made sure to give me a nod, which I did appreciate.

She pointed at me with her thumb. "Right now, we're talking about why we don't have children."

"Oh," the other guy said. "Shit. Sorry."

"You?" the necklace guy said. "Becky J?"

Paula shrugged.

One said, "Man, you can have whatever you want."

"Well," she said, "we're talking about it. I mean right now."

When the guy looked at me, I turned up my palms.

He said, "Hell. Well, good luck. I mean it. Look, we'll be at Le Tub tonight. It's up there, close to Lauderdale. They make great burgers."

Paula mouthed, Thank you. She nodded and the men began to walk away, along the surf. She said, "They know I'm not that goddamn girl. They're just telling me if I hung out with them I could be whoever I wanted to be. We look like a couple of hicks out here." Her voice sounded dry. The two men headed back in the direction of the hairless man, who stood in the surf with his arms crossed.

"This is their turf," I said. "Maybe out here, they feel like they know what they want."

Paula said, "I'm going to go swimming now. You mind?" She stood. She unzipped her shorts, loosened them, let them fall. She wore a thong and I thought she was going to peel that away, too, but she didn't. She moved for the surf and eased her way into the water. She didn't turn to look in my direction, and once she was out there deep enough, she laid out flat, so just her head and her toes were above the surface. I could make out the orange in her shirt and I couldn't help but think of a huge goldfish.

I guessed that she was angry about something other than those guys hitting on her, though I couldn't say what exactly. Maybe she'd had real hopes for me at one point. We were happy when we moved in together in that old shotgun house on Pine Ridge Road. A company house we'd been told, built for steel workers, though the mill had lost thousands of those over the years. We could feel the heartache in that house, the decades of unhappy couples, people stuck in lives they couldn't escape. We'd held up a silver crucifix to that. Business at the track had been fading, it might've been the least surprising news in the history of the world when they announced the place would be closing. Winter was around the corner and she'd be heading for Cleveland. She floated in the ocean now, her face up to the sun, and perhaps she was thinking about those very things.

She stayed out there, and at one point she turned her head in my direction. She watched me in an intent way, and I supposed then I had no idea what she was thinking about. Could it have to do with her and me? I thought about what I could do to surprise her, to change things. Take off my clothes? I watched her and she watched me. It was odd and it went on for a minute. I shook my head and smiled at her. When I did, I thought she smiled back.

I thought, *Children?*

After this, I bowed my head and when I looked up again, she had risen out of the water. She stood close by, dripping, and I held up her shorts. She clutched the ends of her hair and squeezed them. Her wet clothes clung to her, and right then I felt like telling her I loved her. Though I already felt she knew as much.

"Thanks," she said as she took her shorts. She pulled her hair behind her head and squeezed it again. "Why don't you find work here? I mean, at Tropical Park? I watched you while I was out there. I thought, you know, this place does seem to agree with Henry in a way." Paula stuck her hands on her hips and looked out to the ocean. "Water's cold," she said.

"I could probably pitch out stalls, rub horses." My eyes went out to the ocean, too. "I could do that and then come out here every evening. I could say 'I made it.' But my guess is that it wouldn't feel that way."

Paula crouched down. Her face was wet and shining and her eyes seemed large. "I'm sorry about sending your money home like that. That was unrealistic. I wish I hadn't done that now."

I wondered if she could be deciding whether or not I ought to get one more chance. "I'll probably be relieved when we get back to Steelage and the envelope arrives in the mail," I said.

She turned her shoulders, looked out to the water. Then back to me. "What are you going to do?"

"I was thinking Sportsman's Park. In Cicero. You know where I'm talking about?"

"Just outside Chicago. Got friends there?"

No one that I know of, I thought. But you never really knew that until you were at that place. I wound up not answering.

"You ready?" she said. The white sun burned like a spotlight in the sky beyond her and I pulled myself up. Without a word, we began to walk in the direction of the hotel. We didn't talk until we were past the *Beware* sign, and right after that she said, "See anything at the races you like today?"

I said, "Yeah. Sure."

"Maybe I'll go with you. I got, like, a four-hundred-dollar cash limit on my ATM."

"Yeah, well, I am pretty much tapped."

"Right," she said. "First thing, though. I'm taking a shower."

* * *

While Paula showered, I sat up in bed and read the *Racing Form*. In one way, it felt like just another day in my life and I tried to appreciate that. A difference would be that we were going to Tropical Park; it might not have been Hialeah, but it was still one of the better ones going. The infield had an emerald-green turf course for the horses to race over. Near the tote board they had a man-made koi pond with a little crescent-shaped wooden bridge over it. From our place in the grandstand, yesterday, Paula had said she could see the fish when they swam close to the surface. I'd squinted, couldn't make them out. Palm trees lined the backstretch and beyond them were apartment buildings; one had to be forty stories. At Steelage, the closed mill was just a mile or so from the barn area. A dark concoction of dead smokestacks and abandoned sheds. In the distance stood the dark, craggy outline of Hastings Mountain. When I thought about the future of the place, I supposed the people who had been born there would be the ones likely to stay, if only because it was the one life they knew. Paula and I had sat in the Tropical grandstand for a time yesterday, and in between races I'd imagined what kind of life I might have in a place like Miami. Now, I thought, what if she hadn't sent away my money? Would I really have gone seven-grand on something today? For whatever reason, this just didn't seem like the time for that. I supposed she was right. This should be a vacation.

The shower water stopped, and Paula stayed in there for what seemed like a long time afterward. She'd wiped the steam from the mirror with a towel and looked at herself nude. I pictured her doing this, that's what I mean to say. I could picture what she saw, but, of course, I couldn't tell at all what she would be thinking. I hadn't been joking earlier when I told her I sometimes visualized her as pregnant. I thought she would look good, but I also wondered what else I would think about. I had never really talked seriously about having children with anyone I'd dated, not even with the one woman I'd been engaged to. Paula was a tall woman who looked good in everything. She stood in front of a mirror and I read the *Racing Form*. We understood how to reassure ourselves.

When Paula stepped out of the bathroom (finally), she had dressed for the track. She worked on her wet hair with a towel. She wore ankle-length Capri pants, a sleeveless blue blouse, navy espadrilles. "Your turn," she said. I showered fast and I didn't need to stand in front of the mirror for long. We had to hurry if we were going to make the daily double.

On the way, we spotted a Wells Fargo and pulled in to the drive-thru. The ATM was on my side, so Paula passed her debit card over, told me the PIN code, something she hadn't revealed before. I held the money over to her and she counted out five twenties for herself, then passed back the rest. "I feel like getting drunk today," she said. "You don't mind, do you?" I gave a laugh and said of course not.

Once I paid our admission and we were walking under the shadow of the grandstand, Paula headed directly for a bar. I stopped a few feet from there, heard her ask for a Bloody Mary. She didn't bother to see if I wanted anything. But she knew that when I went to the races I didn't drink. That was the fastest way on earth to the poor house. We decided to make our way to the second floor of the grandstand, close to where we'd been the day before. We watched a couple of races from there. I tried to get a feel for things. She went to get another Bloody Mary.

When the horses walked onto the track for the fourth race post parade, I said, "This probably would have been the race, right here. The seven horse, Birdcage, that little bay with the orange saddle towel. Fourteen to one right now. My bet would've dropped it down to ten to one, no worse."

"Seventy grand," she said. "If."

"That's right."

She seemed dreamy, which I believed had been the point of the drinks. After this race, maybe I'd have one, too. Paula said, "So, how would your nerves be right this second?"

"Brutal."

"Then, why?"

I said, "It's what I can think of."

The next thing she said was, "We had plenty of good days, you and me."

"We did." The fourth would be at six furlongs over the dirt track, for horses that had never won a race previously. A fairly nominal event on the card. Yet it might've been a race that told me a lot. If the race turned out badly, maybe it would have me believing again that my life had turned out to be a disappointment. I'd learned any number of things, but the knowledge was meaningless, had never added up to anything and never would. If my horse won, it would be a validation of my way of living. I'd believe, for a while anyway, that I was still on the right path. At the moment, I couldn't decide that if where I was right now meant I'd lost too much in my life or had won just enough.

"Two minutes to post," she said. "Shouldn't you go back

and bet a little, anyway?"

"I guess." I felt myself start to stand, but then my calves felt sore or something and I sat down again. I peeked at the *Form*. What had I missed out on here? If this horse was such a great play, why did it have these long odds? A wave of doubt crashed over me. I'd lost my will. This happened on occasion, too. The horses were on the backstretch, walking in a line for the starting gate. Making a bet on this horse, for whatever reason, just didn't seem like the right thing. Paula seemed curious. She watched me.

"Hell, Henry, I'm going to bet it."

"Go ahead," I said.

I sat by myself as the horses went into the gate. I didn't know if Paula left so I could watch the race alone. I didn't know if she'd get her bet down in time. The gates opened and the horses sprang forward. The race caller said the names of the leaders, but his voice sounded like he was way out on the ocean. After a furlong, the horse with the orange saddle towel, Birdcage, settled in mid-pack. I had one distinct want then: for this horse to lose. Get into traffic trouble, blow the turn, throw a shoe. Anything. Just lose. *What if Paula hadn't sent my money home? What if she and I could live in a penthouse?* That kind of thing could just go on and on.

Midway on the turn, the seven made a bid along the inside. A path had cleared, and it picked up one horse after the next. A spot on the rail opened up at the top of the stretch, but the horses in front kept running hard, and Birdcage couldn't keep up. With a furlong left, the horse appeared to be tiring; it was done, out of gas. My heart was beating hard throughout the race and when it was over, my eyes burned. It was like I'd really had something riding on it.

The tote board said that the eight horse, the first-place finisher, had closed at odds of sixty to one. Immediately, I checked the *Form*. The eight had finished up the track in its two previous starts, but those were grass races in Canada. It was trying dirt racing for the first time today. If I hadn't been so consumed with this all-or-nothing business, I probably would've noticed that beforehand. I lived for horses like that.

Paula returned and sat by me, showed me her ticket, which was twenty to win on number seven. I took it from her and I supposed she thought I'd tear it up or something. For a second, I thought about kissing her, but I didn't do that, either. I looked at the ticket and thought of the envelope, with my name in her handwriting, that would arrive after we got back to West Virginia. I would open the envelope and there would be a cashier's check for $7,000.00. Maybe I'd just think of her as an angel.

My eyes went out to the tote board, to the massive payoffs. There wouldn't be anything like this the rest of the day. Long shots like this came in quite infrequently and you were wasting your time if you believed otherwise.

Paula could read things clearly enough. "Feel like staying?" she said.

I didn't say anything, which was enough of an answer for her. I didn't know what else to do with her ticket, so I stuck it in my pocket. I'd hang on to it, probably with the idea that one day I might look at it and start to change the way I was doing things.

On the way out, Paula walked ahead of me. There wasn't any hurry. Soon enough, it would be time to start packing. I thought about what I'd brought, two pairs of pants, two button-downs, socks, a couple of t-shirts. Some part of me had known we that wouldn't be in paradise for long, that seemed obvious enough. But even if I wasn't going to stay, at least I could say I knew what it had been like.

Selection

Julia needs a few things. It's a Sunday morning and she's been up for a while. Chapstick, sugar, baguette. Her husband, Bobby, who is closer to her father's age than her own, sits in the living room, watching political talk shows. He's already said to the TV, "This guy's never told the truth in his whole life." Then, "Oh, my god, I knew this was going to happen." They've been married for going on nine years. He'll watch TV into the afternoon. She checks on him, and he says, "Heineken, sweetheart. Thank you."

"Bye!" she says.

"Be careful," he says.

After she closes the front door, she surveys the frozen grass of her front lawn, the silent street. She feels despair, which is not unusual. Though this time she says, "I don't love you, Bobby. I truly do not. I never have, and I never will." She walks for her Benz S-Class, feels the grass break under her sneakers. If he had said something besides *Heineken*...had asked for a Laurie Anderson CD or a Harvey Pekar comic, she might've smiled in relief at the effort. She might not have had to say *I don't love* you while looking out on their neighborhood on a cold winter morning. He could've spared her that. Outside of what she has to have, Julia doesn't want anything.

When Julia pulls into the lot at Churchill's Convenience Market, she sees her mother's Lincoln parked in a slot outside the entrance. The store has a nice of variety of pet foods and a better-than-anyone-would've-guessed wine selection. There's an open space next to her mother's car. Julia hesitates. She hasn't planned on seeing her mother, but now it feels like Julia's been looking for her. She loves her mother, but she's angry with her mother over a good many things. Overall, it's not surprising that Julia has wound up living only a few blocks from her parents. She sits on the hood of the Benz in her not-quite-warm-enough peacoat, dangles her legs over the wheel-well. She lights up a cigarette, stares up at the colorless sky. She exhales and watches her smoke float, vanish.

In the corner of her eye, she catches the opening of the glass door to the market. She drops her cigarette to the section of pavement, then she slides down, touches her sneakers to the ground. She turns, gives a forced smile in the direction of her mother. "Hey. Everything okay?" her mother says as she approaches. Her silver hair is tied back; earmuffs rest around her collar like a pair of Beats.

"I just wanted a cigarette," Julia says. "Before I went in."

Her mother moves closer to the passenger door of the Lincoln, reaches for the handle. "Of course."

"I don't love my husband," Julia says. "I never have."

Her mother hesitates. Her back is to Julia. Her mother opens the door, places the plastic sack she's been carrying on the seat. She has her head bowed when she turns and says, "Well, why'd you marry him?" When she looks at Julia, Julia focuses on her pale blue eyes.

"Money," Julia says.

"My daughter?"

"Mom. Mother." Julia's honesty feels liberating, and she knows she's made her mother feel a little worse. She reaches for her mother's elbow to steady them both. Julia's voice is quiet when she says, "What'd you get?"

"Cabernet, batteries, Q-tips."

"For me, it's usually like three things, too. That gets me in the car, three things."

Her mother pulls on leather gloves. "Julia," she says. "What's going on?"

"I told you. I don't love Bobby. Before I left this morning, I asked him what he wanted from the store...even when I could've guessed. I've been thinking about it...I'm not getting him any Heineken and if he asks me about it, I'm going to turn off that TV set and tell him I don't love him. And because I'll tell him when he's doing nothing, he'll tell me he doesn't love me, either. Later, when he's starting to think about work tomorrow, he'll walk in to where I am and say he didn't mean it. He'll say that when he's by himself, he just hates everything. He'll say, 'Tell me you didn't mean it, either.' I pulled in here and saw your car and I almost drove off because I knew if I stopped I'd tell you all this. But maybe you already knew. It was just a matter of when I said it." She eyes her mother, who regards Julia coolly.

"Feelings come and go, sweetheart."

"I know that," Julia says. "I knew you knew." Her voice is quieter when she says, "Hey, you look kinda cold there, Mom."

"Would you like to get a coffee with me?"

Julia feels like hugging her but doesn't. "No," she says. "Too late in the morning for coffee." She puts on what feels like a defeated-looking smile.

"Julia...sometimes. You can be... Look, I think Bobby has been good for you. He knows how to relax."

"He's sitting in his chair right now, swearing at senators."

"None of us are suffering personally, dear. Goodness."

"Mom, I'll see you later, okay? It's fine. Like you just said...emotions don't last. Practically none of them. In a couple of days, I'll make a cake. I'll drive over to see you and Daddy."

"Well, I'd like that, we'll look forward to it. Listen, it's just so gray out. We need to plan a trip to Miami. Stay at the Sea View for a week. Let's talk about that soon...when you come over. Julia, you're a grown woman. You needed to say what you've said. Now, perhaps you understand something. You realize...you should always talk to me first, yes? It's good we ran into each other this morning. Shouldn't you be wearing a hat, sweetheart?"

"I'm heading in right now." She leans over, makes a kiss-sound next to her mother's cheek.

From inside the door of the market, Julia watches as her mother backs out. Julia scolds herself. Here was her mother just running an errand and Julia hit her with all of this. But then Julia thinks, You can't really call me a bitch for telling her something she already knew.

She steps aside when someone says, "Pardon me." A guy in jeans, wool jacket, a child holding his hand. They step out and when the kid turns and looks back at Julia, she gives the child a wave. She takes in a breath, turns and faces the aisles. Now what did she come in here for? She knows the store, knows what they sell, so whatever it is will be here. Heineken, she doesn't want to get that, but she probably will. If she forgets, he'll gripe. He'll say, All I do for you and… It's always better to just give him what he wants, especially if that's all it is.

First, she'll shop for herself. She winds up standing in front of the section marked *French Reds*. The words are handwritten on an index card taped to the wall just above the shoulder-high shelf. She spots a bottle of Louis Jadot, Pouilly-Fuissé. She swirls around, says in the direction of the cashier, "Hey, Hazel, when did you start carrying this, the Pouilly-Fuissé?"

The woman behind the register adjusts her eyeglasses, leans forward. "We've had that for a while," she says. "Pretty sure."

"Man, you all think of everything." She says this in a murmur as she faces the shelf. She draws in another measured breath, then reaches for the bottle.

At the Democrat Museum in Madisonville, Kentucky

My mother and I are sitting at opposite ends of her kitchen table. I drove up from Memphis this morning, at the urging of my two sisters, who say they're getting worried. They want me to call afterwards, give my impressions. My mother and I are wearing face masks. She's a cradle-to-grave Democrat, used to feeling optimistic. Her hair is white.

One wall in the kitchen is covered with clipped-out newspaper and magazine articles from *The Madisonville Messenger*, *Louisville Courier-Journal*, *Time*, *Newsweek*. Upbeat pieces on local celebrations, Derby winners, Olympic athletes, the St. Louis Cardinals. There are articles about Hillary, the Obamas. I spot just a couple on Joe Biden, and I know she still holds a mild grudge because Barack selected him as a running mate over Hillary. I felt like it was a misplaced view; Biden was super-qualified to be vice-president. It was an argument we had years ago. She's been doing this since I was a kid, cutting out and taping up news stories. She'd put them up on the fridge and after the fridge was covered, she'd go to a wall. They had a little grease-fire here, right after W was reelected, something to do with burning pork, and the walls got scorched. She had to start over after that.

At the moment, my mother has the storm door propped open, and when the breeze flows in through the top half of the screen door it rustles the articles, many of which have yellowed. It makes me think that winter is nearby, even if it's only September.

My mother says she's heard on the radio that Kamala Harris campaigns in tennis shoes. She wants to know if it's true.

I confirm this, I've seen photos. Chuck Taylors, I say, probably sounding gruff because of the mask. I can get you a pair. High-tops if you want them.

She says, Don't waste your money.

My sisters have bought her face masks; all bright, solid colors. She's chosen a purple one for my visit. She has weak lungs, emphysema, and, as she jokes, is on more meds than a megachurch preacher undergoing a seven-year IRS audit.

I'm wearing a surgical-type mask, which I realize now is a lousy choice.

I'm hit with a memory that's fifty-plus years old: My mother taking my sisters and me to a public park in Tampa, where we lived at one time, so we could see an LBJ motorcade as it passed by. When it did, the tinted windows were up on the presidential limousine and there were little American flags sticking up from the four corners of the hood. We waved like crazy and it disappeared in the distance.

I am no spring chicken myself. I sense that one reason my mother keeps staring at me is because of how gray my hair has become.

My mother is a good mother, and while more or less staying on the subject of politics, I remind her about that time in Tampa when we waited for LBJ's motorcade. I don't mention it, but I wonder if her idea there was to make us feel like we were really part of America and proud of it and so on. Naturally, we were children.

I'm testing her, too, to be perfectly honest about it.

She says it didn't happen.

I offer the motorcade details, the little American flags.

She says, Motorcade...are you thinking of Kennedy?

I was a year old when Kennedy was killed. I don't need to remind her of this. I say, It wasn't Kennedy.

She says, The day Kennedy was assassinated in his motorcade was on a Friday.

Right, I say. This must've been three or four years later. When Daddy was training horses in Tampa.

Your daddy was a bum, she says.

I'm aware of that, I say.

Call your sisters, she says. Go on, call them. For a second, I think she means so they can verify the thing about my father. (Which they would.) But I get it, she's talking about the LBJ motorcade.

* * *

My sisters, Kelly and Beth, are talkative. Beth, my younger sister, would've been a little baby at the time I'm thinking of, so she isn't the one to ask. I lean back in my chair, tug down my mask. I dial Kelly, who lives in Louisville; I told her yesterday that I was driving up here this morning. Hey, I say.

Everything all right? she says.

Yeah, we're just sitting here, I say.

What do you think? she says. I've just told her that my mother and I are together. I look to my mother for sympathy, even though it's her I'm trying to keep this part of the discussion from. *Like, does Kelly ever listen?* We're talking about LBJ, I say.

What?

Not about him so much as that time we went to see his motorcade pass. Do you remember that?

Hmm, Kelly says. What's the point of contention exactly?

It's not a point of contention, I say. *Jesus*, I think. I say, It's something I remember...

But her memory isn't..., Kelly says.

I say, Do you...?

She says, Sure. We had that old Chrysler station wagon. Daddy wasn't there, probably out chasing some barmaid. We dropped the tailgate and we sat and waited. For a long time as I recall. Hours.

I don't remember that part, I say.

I do, she says. And the motorcade, it zoomed by.

Right, I say. I have that, too. Okay, well that solves it.

That was all? she says.

I say, Like I said, we couldn't decide if it happened or not. I was starting to wonder if I dreamed it.

How do you think she is overall? my sister says. Is she wearing her mask? She doesn't like wearing her mask.

Oh? I turn up one palm, as if to say to my mother, *Does she ever stop?*

Kelly says, She doesn't want to wear it in the grocery store or anything.

I'd like my sister to lighten up. *The scandal, her not wearing a mask...*I think about saying this, but I catch myself, realize I'll sound like a bastard son of Kellyanne Conway.

I guess I am starting to understand something.

Okay, thanks, I'll talk to you later, I say. I hang up on her right after that.

I say to my mother, She says you don't want to wear your mask to the grocery store. You're wearing your mask with me here, but you don't want to wear it there? I don't understand.

The store makes me wear it, so what does it matter? she says. You'll try to make me feel guilty, so I put it on. She shrugs and says, It's not like the air's worth breathing anyway.

We're alive, I say. The air is okay.

It's just how I feel, she says. What did your sister say?

I say, Kelly says the LBJ thing happened. She says we waited for hours. Knowing my mother can use a little boost, I say, You've always been really good about that, you know what I mean?

You mean waiting? she says and even from under the mask it sounds hurt. She knows that isn't it and I wait for her to rebound. She says, Well, I was raised that way. My father shook hands with Kennedy once, when he came to campaign here.

I'm thinking we still might not be talking about the same thing. What I meant was that she always wanted us to be positive about life and the country we lived in. She might be talking about being an unwavering Democrat. *A good Democrat will wear their mask*, I want to say. I guess the point is that she's eighty-five years old and is too depressed to protect herself. I understand why my sisters are worried.

I say, What can I do?

In a moment, she says, You waved at LBJ's motorcade. It's gone now. She reaches up to rub her forehead; her thumb gets hung up in the strap that goes around her ear. She readjusts her mask. She takes in a measured breath, then another. I'm okay, she says. You don't worry about me…it's coming back to me, that motorcade. Your sister was right. We waited all day for that. It sped right on by. Guess they didn't want to take any chances. Weren't sure they were among friends. She and I wind up watching one another. She says, I am glad to see ya.

I say, Any time you want company…here isn't that far away for me.

Hmm, she says.

I know, I say.

It's all right, she says.

I say, What about those shoes? My mother doesn't say anything. So I say to her something she used to say to us a million times over. I say, It'll get better. It sounds strange, coming from me. And not terrifically convincing.

She says, Sonny, take down your mask again. It won't hurt anything, so I do it. Like my mother would ever place me in danger. She says, You look tired. I want you to go upstairs and take a nap before you drive back.

Maybe I'll just spend the night, if that's all right, I say.

That's all right. How's, ah, is it Lauren? she says.

Laura, I say. I haven't spoken to her in a while, Mom. I fix my mask back over the bridge of my nose.

We sit in the quiet of the kitchen. It's the middle of September and there's no breeze. It'll come. Because I know she follows them, I ask her about the Cardinals, if they're going to make a run in the playoffs.

She seems to think on it, though maybe her mind wants to focus on something other than baseball. I've never followed it too closely. I wind up thinking of my old room upstairs, the window I looked out every day when I was a teenager. Tomorrow morning, I'll awaken, and the sunlight will probably be flooding in through that window. Almost certainly, I'll lie there and try to imagine what I used to wonder about, how I wanted my life to turn out, if what I have is even close to that. I'm telling myself, *In some ways…*, but of course that's what you have to say. The sunlight will be pouring in. I'll head downstairs, have coffee with my mother, and then it'll be time to drive back to Memphis.

My mother says, Maybe next year.

Hmm? I say.

Her expression, from what I can see of it, seems a bit curious. The Cardinals? she says.

I want to joke with her about always saying the same thing. But more than anything, I appreciate it now. I say, Yeah, that would be great.

It might be pointless, but I've decided that when I get back to Memphis, I'll get on Amazon and order her a pair of Chuck Taylors. (I can imagine my sisters' reaction: *This is your solution? Converse?*) It's possible that when the box arrives, she'll remove the lid, eye the shoes and laugh a quiet laugh, if only because she'll know where they came from.

Passport Office

On a Saturday morning in June, Graham and Melanie Bonnet are having takeout breakfast sandwiches from Fanfreluche, a vegetarian restaurant in their neighborhood. The kitchen table in their fourth-floor condo is by a window that looks down to the street, and the street is marked with a line of orange cones for a 10k sponsored by the Atlanta Track Club. Graham hasn't spotted a runner in a while and he wonders if the race has concluded. The cones haven't been collected. His thoughts drift. "I saw a billboard yesterday advertising Alberta. Banff National Forest. Ice-blue lakes, snowy-top mountains. Maybe we should go there for a while."

She says, "I'd have to check my schedule."

The cardboard container in front of him holds his half-eaten, mock sausage patty with cashew cheese sauce on flatbread. He says, "I like it when they add a touch of clove. I don't taste that today. I'm about finished with this."

"Me, too." She wears a vanilla-colored t-shirt and khaki shorts. She's slender, with gray-blond hair. Her recent promotion in Emory's HR department has turned into longer hours.

"I mean griping. I'm going to be...proactive." He knows it's a word she likes to emphasize.

Melanie says, "I'd love to go to Banff. Might need to get our passports renewed. They've probably expired. You have to renew every ten years."

"Where are they?"

"Pretty sure I gave you mine after we came back from Barcelona."

He tosses his paper napkin at the container. "Let's see...that was when…seven years ago? That's the last time we went to Europe?" His throat feels dry. "Suppose we just want to get out of this country for good? Don't you ever think of doing that? I won't need permission from some idiot executive vice-president, believe me. But we'd need our passports."

"Well, we're not going to leave for good this week because we've got the protest at the state capitol on Thursday. Voters' rights."

"Is that this Thursday?" She doesn't need to answer. "We want to have current passports, Melanie. That's ridiculous we let that slide. We need to have options. Our lives can't be just this." Her expression turns less patient. "Do you mind if I go look for them real quick? While it's on my mind?"

"Go right ahead."

He heads upstairs, for his office. The passports aren't in his desk, so he moves for their closet. He goes through the shoeboxes where she keeps the vital documents and photos of her family back in Vicksburg. He looks through the photos, winds up slipping one in the pocket of his shirt. He finds a manila envelope with their marriage license and their birth certificates and returns to the table downstairs with the envelope, even though it isn't what he's looking for. "All there is," he says, holding the envelope over to her. "Oh, and this." He removes the photo from his shirt pocket. In the photo, Melanie is a teenager. She's in her bare feet, wears cutoff shorts and a gray polo, and sits on the hood of her mother's lima-bean-colored Falcon with her knees bent, her arms folded around them. He says, "Dixie belle."

"Bones and freckles," she says, in a murmur. "Man, I did love to floor that old heap down the river highway. Put it back in the box, please…where it's junior year forever."

He tucks the photo in the pocket of his shirt. They look over their own birth certificates. These are simple documents. Graham's complete name is typed out in capital letters. Born in Owensboro County, Kentucky, September 14, 1963. He can't help but think of the quiet house in the country where he'd been raised. Melanie's parents lived in Mississippi and were in their late thirties when they had her, she was the "surprise." He and Melanie had been married in New Orleans on July 22, 1992, at the city courthouse. They needed two witnesses and the judge, Dominic Altry, had standbys ready: his wife, Ruby, and a secretary, one Jane Borello. Graham and Melanie had been grad students at Mississippi State and couldn't afford anything more than the JOP wedding and one-night honeymoon in New Orleans. They were deeply in love. Looking over the documents turns Graham thoughtful. He says, "We'll feel better if our passports are valid. Let's make that a priority."

"Shouldn't we have a place we want to go?"

"We will. We just want to be ready."

In the days that follow, the passports don't turn up. Melanie says she's looked everywhere. Graham opens drawers, brings down box after box from closet shelves. He remembers the trip to Barcelona; they each contracted a stomach virus, and this kept them from exploring the city. They spent most of the time in their neat rental apartment on the Mediterranean. In the afternoons, they sat on the balcony chairs and looked out to the sea. One of them would have to duck back inside. By the end of the week they were each feeling better and joking about it, saying maybe next time they'd take a walk *on* the beach. Then it was time to fly home. Back in Atlanta, they discussed future destinations: Johannesburg, Vienna, Tokyo. In recent years, they'd been to Boston, Charleston, and the Alabama Gulf Coast. Shorter trips, just a few days. They're glad for any traveling. Work keeps them occupied. They've been going along with it.

On Thursday, they both skip lunch in order to participate in the protest outside the state capitol. She finds him in the smallish crowd, he's a tall man, 6'4", with wavy auburn-and-white hair. The rally leader, an African American war veteran in combat fatigues, stands on a lawn of the capitol on a blazing afternoon. He speaks into a bullhorn. "The local government are traitors to the constitution! Let 'em know it every minute of every day. Let them hear your voices!" Melanie and Graham chant with the crowd, "De-moc-ra-cy! De-moc-ra-cy!"

Back at the condo that evening, he does the research, discovers they'll have to renew their passports in person. He explains this to her while they're sitting up in bed. She's wearing the sky-blue nightgown with spaghetti straps and this can, but does not always, mean she would like some attention. He notices the blinds are closed tight. They're both feeling a bit fired up from the rally. He says, "I've been thinking about it. Getting a new passport, that's always been a good thing for us. It's exciting, it's cool."

"I'll find the time." She reaches for his hand. She brings it to her, kisses it. "Let's talk about something else."

He's been married to Melanie for twenty-seven years. Making love to her is easy tonight. He doesn't go to sleep thinking about passports. He thinks about their honeymoon in New Orleans. The room they had was adjacent to an office and a noisy copy machine. They slept on and off. Tonight, the sounds of her nearing-climax gasps remain in his ears. When he awakens on Friday morning, it's after seven, not long before the alarm on his watch will sound. He can see the sunlight at the edges of the closed blinds in their bedroom. Melanie seems to be sleeping, her head lolled back on the double-stacked pillows. His body is tired, and it shouldn't be this way. Yesterday, he got up, dressed, went to work, took a late lunch to protest scary and obnoxious local policies concerning voter registration, came home and made love to his wife, something he'd done, by his instant estimate, a couple of thousand times now. "Mel," he says.

"Yes?" she says, in a voice that sounds close to wide awake.

"Let's skip work today. I'll make you pancakes. We'll take a long drive. No news, no turning on the radio."

"You okay?"

"Fine. I don't want you to feel like you don't have a lot to look forward to. I know all that's happening out there...this is hard on everybody."

When she speaks, her eyes are open and she's looking at the peach-colored ceiling. "My lack of imagination. That bothers me. That makes me feel powerless. Cornered."

"You have a wonderful imagination."

"I find myself jumping to worst-case scenarios. More often than not. This bothers me. I get it, where you're coming from. We can't move away from America yet, though. I'm not moving anywhere until each one of the shitty bastards running this country is out of office. Until every last ounce of their human slime is gone. Then, we'll talk."

"New passports have always made us feel better. We can talk about places we want to see. We don't need billboards...once we finish applying for passports, I'll spring for dinner."

She kisses his cheek. "Time for me to get up."

* * *

They agree to meet on Tuesday afternoon at the Midtown passport office. He leaves work, drives in that direction. It's 98 degrees and the traffic on West Peachtree crawls along. He spots a portable electronic board with a blinking arrow: three lanes are funneled into one by construction. There are orange cones but not a hardhat in sight. The parking area for the passport office is beyond the post office lot. The lots are separated by eight-foot-high chain-link fencing; three strands of new-looking barbwire are strung above the top of the fence line. The gate's on wheels and has been pushed open, so he drives on through.

The passport office is air conditioned, and when Graham shows the clerk his filled-out form, she hands him a numbered ticket from the plastic dispenser. The waiting area beyond her features rows of chairs facing the line of cubicles along the far wall. Beyond the cubicles are vertical panels: cherry-painted walls alternating with ceiling-to-floor windows. A digital display is attached to the ceiling above each cubicle; three of the displays are dark, the others read 84, 77, 86. The number Graham holds is 94. Between the waiting area and the line of cubicles are three support poles, each one bearing a plasma-screen TV.

When Melanie arrives, it's a few minutes after three. She takes her place next to him without a word. He shows her his ticket and she shows him hers, which says 101. She sticks that in a pocket of her purse and brings out a Ziplock bag of baby carrots; Graham's hungry, but he doesn't want one. Other applicants are scattered about in the seating area, some tapping at the screens of their phones, though one man in beige coveralls is leaned back in his chair, sleeping with his mouth open, his arms crossed in front of him. The panels of ceiling-to-floor windows beyond the cubicles hold whitish light.

Graham doesn't watch a lot of TV and isn't thrilled with the prospect of sitting through a talk show or some staged reality thing with Jerry Springer. When the commercials end, there's a scene from a soap opera. He says, in a murmur, "Is that Scotty Baldwin?" He turns to Melanie, perhaps appearing a touch incredulous. She's crunching on a carrot, reading something on her phone.

"What's that?" she says. She glances around the waiting area.

"Scotty Baldwin, up there. That's *General Hospital.*" Graham is squinting in the direction of the TV screen. "I can't believe it. How long has he been on this show?"

"Want me to look it up for you?"

Graham holds up his switched-off phone while turning back to the TV. "Look at him. He's never learned to brush his hair. I told you about this, didn't I? The whole *General Hospital* thing with me? Back when I was a teenager and my grandparents used to watch it all the time?" He is speaking in just above a whisper. "I'd go over there to cut their grass, and after the work was done, we'd watch *General Hospital.* After Pap's stroke he couldn't use his left hand or his left arm very well, so he couldn't work in the yard…I'd zip over there on my bike. They'd pay me ten bucks a day but we'd always stop at three so we could go inside, into the air conditioning, and watch *General Hospital.*"

"I remember your grandfather."

"You only knew him when he had cancer," Graham says. "He had the stroke while he was in his mid-fifties. He lived on Pall Malls and Jim Beam. He ground himself into bits to make his business go. After the stroke, he decided to turn the business over to my old man. Pap and Gran moved into this ranch-style house because he couldn't go up and down stairs too well. You know all this. You should know all this." He hopes that he doesn't sound irritable. Her eyes are on the TV screen.

He says, "When I was a kid, I became interested in the show…in this ironic way. I paid attention to the story, but I think I was really trying to understand what was happening with my grandparents. Before his stroke, he was a vital guy, out making sales calls every day, and then he wound up watching soap operas, smoking his Pall Malls…the doctor told him to stop smoking but he wasn't going to do that. My grandparents would let me have cigarettes…I was just a fourteen, fifteen-year-old kid. I think they just wanted me to hang around with them. After the stroke, I think it was just him and her, a lot of the time. My old man was busy supposedly, running the company. He preferred sitting in bars, going to the track." He wants her to see he's smiling; she slides her finger across the screen on her phone.

"Scotty Baldwin is played by Kin Shriner…who has played him for…you're right, the last forty-two years. He joined the show when he was seventeen…"

On TV, Scotty Baldwin is having dinner with someone at a restaurant. He's arguing with a woman who is considerably younger than him, something to do with a property investment. The sound from the TV is too low to hear every word. Graham says, "The funny thing was, when I got to college, I kept watching the show. For a while, anyway. It was a popular show, with Luke and Laura. Rick Springfield played a doctor. I wanted to go to school further away than I did, but Memphis State was the only place that would take me. I'd never been much of anywhere before then. I'd been a hotshot basketball player in high school...I was all right then. I tried out for the freshman team at Memphis, that was another world... My roommate had a TV, there were only three or four channels. We knew it was all bullshit, but we watched *General Hospital*...to be..."

"Ironic," she says.

"Sure. Once I found a girlfriend, I started to lose interest. This was before you, of course. Then I met you and kind of forgot about it altogether. That's a compliment by the way." They've been speaking in low, semi-secretive voices, even though the nearest applicants are four rows back: a smiling, youthful African American woman and a little boy, who grins wide while sitting up straight in his chair, as if posing for a photo. Graham says, "I never asked them if they felt trapped living in that little ranch house...they would've bullshitted me. They would've said, 'This is the life. No more work, Easy Street.' But it's like the life somebody else imagined for them...and not completely." The screen changes to a commercial for a fast-food place. He pictures himself back with his grandparents, watching TV. The little ranch-style house had been convenient for his grandparents, and as things turned out they'd lived there the rest of their lives. He dreams of them now; in these dreams, sometimes they ask why he hasn't been by to visit more often.

Lung cancer killed both his grandparents; they went six months apart. Not long after this, his parents had to move into the little ranch house. His father lost the family business, as well as the house Graham had been raised in. His parents collect social security, and when Graham calls to see what they're up to, they like to talk about what they've been watching on TV. During one of their recent conversations, his father cautioned Graham about the long hours he worked. Enjoy your life, son, his father said. In the end, we're all gonna wind up in the same place. Graham still isn't certain if his father was talking about the cemetery or heaven. His parents are practicing Catholics, and Graham remembers enough about the sermons from his childhood to know that as far as Catholics are concerned, heaven is far from a sure bet.

Did his father mean the ranch house?

* * *

After Graham completed a four-year degree in business at Memphis State, he pursued post-grad studies in business at Mississippi State. That's where he met Melanie, who at the time was a grad student interested in Labor Relations. She was an amazing lover and they'd wound up eloping to New Orleans. They finished their degrees. They wanted careers; she finally decided on HR, and he settled on hotel management. Looking for work in these fields, they moved to Atlanta. This had been twenty-plus years ago.

In her early forties, Melanie decided to stop taking birth control pills. She was growing wary of side effects; she also had come to believe she was too old to get pregnant. But then one afternoon, as they were having bowls of her homemade French onion soup for lunch, she told Graham she was. She liked to serve a Rhine wine with her onion soup but hadn't brought out the bottle this time, which should have suggested something to him. This would be a crucial moment in their lives, and neither of them had to say that. She told him she wanted to think about what she wanted to do. He said, Melanie, whatever you decide, I'll abide by it. If you want to have it, that's fine. They went the whole week without having wine at dinner. He thought about being a father, how much that might change his life. He thought having a child might bring them joy.

She came to speak to him about it on a Sunday afternoon, in between lunch and dinner. He was stretched out on the bed, reading from a collection of stories by Scott Fitzgerald. She sat on the edge of the bed. She knitted her fingers together. She looked at him squarely and then she spoke, told him she'd made an appointment to have an abortion the day after tomorrow and she wanted him to come with her. He'd already set the book down. He nodded his head, and he said, All right. She said she wanted to explain. She'd been thinking about a lot of things. Part of him felt as if an explanation wasn't necessary, but he remained silent.

Melanie said that when she was growing up in Mississippi, she never dreamed she'd have a life like this. She never thought she'd wind up with a man who wouldn't punch her lights out, or at least threaten to. She thought she'd wind up living in a trailer, pouring vodka into Mountain Dew after she finished her shift at the drywall plant. Even when she was in college, even when they were making love like a couple of wild things in that one-bedroom flat in Starkville, she always wanted to remain realistic. The pursuit of happiness, she felt, was an obvious trap. But as things turned out, she was happy with him, or at least as happy as she was ever going to be. She said she was grateful to him. She felt the world was a sad and wicked place and that she had been lucky, but how did she know a child of hers would be as fortunate? She'd tried to imagine if it were a different time in America, if Bush and Cheney weren't in charge. Would she feel better about having a child? She realized that it didn't matter; JFK or FDR could've been running things.

She said, I'm not too old to have a child, but I simply don't want a child. I already feel well off and I don't want to ask for much more than I have. Maybe this means I'm just some hick kid from Mississippi who doesn't understand all that life has to offer. But I don't care about that. And I don't want to be with anyone else, I'm not looking for a reason to get away from you. Can you understand?

When he spoke, he said, I knew all of this and I didn't. But I should've known everything already, Melanie. I'm glad we're married, whether we have a child or not. He said, You want to get a book and rest here with me?

No, she said. I'm all worked up now. I was actually prepared for a big throwdown.

I've said enough, he said.

You mad?

Maybe a little, he said. I'll probably stay in here for a little while.

Which story are you on?

He picked up the opened book, showed her. "The Curious Case of Benjamin Button."

I'll call you for dinner, she said.

A couple of days later, he drove her to the appointment at the abortion clinic. Later that fall, she decided to have tubal ligation surgery.

The following spring, he put together a ten-day vacation to Berlin for them. They were free to do such things. They stayed in an apartment on the old communist side of the city, a decrepit building that had a newly painted lobby decorated with IKEA furniture. They loved the city, strolled through the Tiergarten almost every afternoon. A couple of years after the Berlin trip was when they went to Barcelona. They spent much of their time together sitting on the balcony, looking out to the Mediterranean.

* * *

On the TV screen, there's an image of the *General Hospital* logo, and the announcer is saying the show will return in just a moment. Commercials follow. At the moment, Graham feels clear on certain things. He's gotten to do far more in his life than he ever dreamed of as a kid, even if these things wouldn't seem extraordinary to anyone else. He knows his life has not gone badly.

He'd never say that, not if it all ended ten minutes from now.

All he can think to do is lean closer to Melanie and say, "I love you."

She's touching at spots on her screen. "I know," she says, her voice quiet.

"Ninety-two!" one of the clerks calls from the cubicle area.

The screen goes from commercial to a scene with another character he recognizes right away: Laura. She was Laura Spencer when married to Luke, and Laura Baldwin way back when she'd been married to Scotty. She's also having dinner at a restaurant with someone, and after a moment they're arguing; of course, it's a soap so there has to be a lot of this. Genie Francis plays Laura, and she can't be but a year or two older than Graham. She might've had some help, but she doesn't look her age. Laura is saying something about the people of Port Charles, they're who she represents…

Graham says, "Laura…a politician?"

The next time Melanie speaks, she says, "Mayor. She's a semi-regular now." She holds up her phone for Graham to see. He accepts it, glances from the phone to the screen, then back again. The restaurant scene ends and the show switches to a scene where a young man and woman are kissing. They pull back, and the guy begins to speak. Their mouths remain close; they're whispering things. Graham imagines they're concocting a plan to leave Port Charles forever.

"Here," he says, holding the phone back to her. "Luke, the guy Laura was married to, he was mayor for a while, I remember that…before he left the show. I don't know how he was qualified to be the mayor, though. He was in the mob, he was a rapist. He raped Laura…she wound up marrying him. I think they got away with it because they were doing a love conquers all thing… Oh, hell, something's coming back to me. One season, Luke and Laura stopped this madman from taking control of the world. They went to some island and this guy had a diamond, I think, that could control the weather. It was called the Ice Princess, the diamond, the crazy guy was going to freeze the whole world…didn't you watch this show at all?" He's smiling, feeling foolish.

"What now?" she says.

"Maybe their ratings were down that year, maybe they just thought they could get away with anything. But this guy, and I don't remember his name, he lived on an island and was in possession of a diamond that could control the weather. He was basically holding the whole world for ransom."

"Sounds prescient to me."

"Oh, well…yeah, I guess it is." He laughs softly. "Who knew? Maybe Laura ran for office on that: 'I know how to shut down a lunatic.'"

Melanie says, "What're the voters like in…where is it?"

"Port Charles." He shrugs. "It's an American town, a small town." He thinks of his grandparents, the light from the TV playing off their bifocals in the darkened living room. "Waiting to be told what they want." He bows his head again, notices his watch. "Look, I need to get back to work. You okay, you still got time?"

"I'll have to work late. It's all right. We're almost there."

When he looks to the TV screen, credits are rolling; they're going by fast, and before he knows it there's the local news, two anchors seated at a desk. It's almost as if they're there to recap the episode. There's an image of President Trump, waving just before he boards Air Force One.

"Fuck you," Melanie says in a normal voice.

"Ninety-four!"

She reaches for the handle of her purse. Graham's on his feet, and he looks to the place where the young woman and child have been sitting. They're gone; then he spots them at a cubicle, the young woman perched forward on her chair, the child standing right by her knees. Graham follows Melanie for the cubicle at the middle of the row, the one that has the counter reading 94.

There are two seats across from the postal worker at the desk. The worker is a middle-aged African American woman wearing a wig of curly hair that's a bit loose at the crown. They hand over their paperwork, which she takes a minute to examine. On her desk are a bowl of peppermints, a credit card reader, a foot-high tripod with a camera affixed to its top.

"Need to see your driver's licenses," she says.

Melanie holds hers over. "I see you in the post office, you helped me last time I bought stamps, I didn't want the ones with the flag. You showed me the stamps with Gregory Hines. Which is better, working here or over there?"

"Here," the woman says, without looking up from the forms. "I get to sit down." When she hands back Melanie's license, she's smiling. "And where are y'all planning on heading?"

Both Graham and Melanie hate it when people are difficult with those who have the this-is-what-I-wound-up-doing jobs; he thinks the worker might get where he's coming from when he says, "Anywhere but here?" She gives him a nice smile and her expression isn't lacking in sympathy.

"I need an actual place." She holds her pen over the form.

"Iceland," Melanie says. "Put Iceland."

It takes Graham a second to realize she's almost certainly making a joke about the Ice Princess season. He says, "Yes, Iceland...good one."

The worker writes out something on each of their applications. "Now, we just need a picture," she says. She nods to Graham, "You're already in front of the background...just lean back a little." He notices the vanilla-toned fabric covering the partition behind him. He sits up, clears his throat. "Smile if you want to," she says. From the corner of his eye, he sees that Melanie is brushing her hair.

For her photo, they have to switch seats. She takes his place, straightens her skirt. She finds a little smile and her picture is taken. The worker then turns the camera and beckons Melanie closer so she can see the image. "I guess," Melanie says. Then they're both looking in Graham's direction.

He sits forward so he can see the digital image of her on the camera screen. He says, "Mel's never taken a bad photo." He sits back.

Melanie says, "He was ready for that one."

The worker gives them a nod of approval. Just for a second it feels as if they're here applying for something else. "Well, that's it," she says. "You'll be getting the new passports in five to seven weeks. That'll be two-eighty for the two of you." She nods to the credit card reader on her desk, and because all of this was Graham's idea, he reaches for his wallet.

When they're outside again, they each have to shield their eyes; Melanie does this with one hand, Graham uses the receipt. Then Melanie's reaching in her purse for her shades. They walk for her Kia, and he says, "Don't give up."

"I haven't," she said, her voice small.

"I'll get dinner," he says. "I said I would."

"No, no. I wanna pay for something. Maybe Lin-Lu's?"

"Sounds good. Make sure they include fortune cookies. They forgot last time..." Then she's in her Kia, waving to him from behind the driver's side window. She's late, she needs to get to work. The tires give a little shriek as Melanie pulls onto West Peachtree. He needs to get back, too.

* * *

The passports arrive in late August, in a single, padded manila envelope. That evening, he gets home late from work; it's nearly eight and she's seated at the kitchen table. She's pushed off her pumps; otherwise, she's in the clothes she left the condo in this morning. The envelope has been opened, the two passports with their navy-blue covers are on the table, along with an opened sleeve of saltines. She's poured herself a glass of red wine. Graham's carrying his briefcase. "Was I supposed to bring home dinner?" he says.

She says, "One of us was, I guess. I just got here ten minutes ago. I thought vaguely of microwaving something."

He takes a seat across from her. "Tell me we have lots of wine left."

"Lots."

"Well, that's something." He supposes the passport closer to him is his. He wishes he hadn't made a fuss about getting these. It's sensible, people need their passports. He reminds himself of this. But it isn't helpful to pretend. He opens the passport, and there's his photo on the first page; he turns the booklet on its side to get a right-side-up look. The cover of his passport is stiff, unbent, non-worn. He thumbs through the pages where the travel stamps can go, notices the backgrounds. There are images of the Liberty Bell, a Bald Eagle, the Statue of Liberty. He closes it, places it back on the table.

Graham decides to stand up, pour himself a glass of wine. He carries the three-quarter-empty glass back to the table. They can talk about their days if they want. They can talk about whatever they feel like. He says, "I'm pretty beat. But it's all right. I want to sit up with you for a while."

"The wine is good," she says.

"It is, actually."

"Thank god."

It's dark outside and headlights move down the street. The window holds the reflections of her and him. "Push those crackers over here," he says.

Secret

Frank Cordero stepped inside Carpaccio's Italian Restaurant and the smiling host, Angel, held up two fingers. "Just me," Frank said. "Takeout. Thank you." He walked over to the bar, ordered a broiled flounder platter to go and a scotch and soda for while he waited. The woman Frank lived with had gone out of town yesterday and he hadn't spoken to anyone since. She frequently worked weekends, said she couldn't do anything about her scheduling. He had this entire Saturday to himself.

Frank's dinner arrived in a Styrofoam shell. He finished his drink and carried the shell back up the street to his condominium. During the walk, his cell phone rang. The ID said the caller was Kelly, his second ex-wife, who now lived in Miami Lakes. She said she'd like to drop in on him, but only if he was alone. He said that he was, decided to leave out the details. Leaving out her details as well, she said she'd be over in a while. He opened the door to his condominium. The long, rectangular living room had ocean blue, wall-to-wall carpeting. The far end of the room was sunken; the blinds there were closed. He carried his dinner to the kitchen, placed it on top of the stove, then opened the lid of the shell to consider the flounder, English peas, and artichoke hearts. When they'd been married, and had lived together in Bal Harbor with his son from his first marriage, the three of them had frequently dined at Carpaccio's. He wondered what she wanted to tell him. It wouldn't be something wonderful. Nonetheless, he was pleased at the prospect of getting to see her. He closed the lid, decided to wait.

A short while later, he heard knocking at the front door. He opened it and Kelly said, "Here I am." He stepped back. She wore a white blouse, caramel-colored jeans, and gold-colored sandals. With both hands, she held on to a small, bright blue purse that somewhat matched the color of her eyes. Her silvery-blond hair hung loose, reached her shoulders. She said, "Is someone living here with you, Frank? I mean, these days?"

"Is it the watercolor?" he said, gesturing to the painting of a city skyline that hung next to the entrance of the bedroom. "For a little while now. A pilot for American," he said. "Charlotte...she's here on and off. Flew out yesterday for Berlin. She talked me into that Marin. Wants to get another. She wants the place to have some, I don't know..."

"We have a problem, Frank," Kelly said, her eyes still traveling about.

"Oh. All right."

"It's Michael."

"Michael."

"Mmm-hmm."

"What'd he do, Kelly?"

She exhaled, she seemed content in a way. He couldn't decide if it was because the condo seemed so familiar. "He called me early this morning," she said. "He owes bookmakers ten or twelve thousand dollars. He said ten at one point, then at another he said twelve. He's got till next Friday to pay them."

"That little bastard."

"Frank," she said. "He's in trouble." She blinked at him. "We know how this turns out. We help. Do you have any wine?"

Kelly always seemed a step or two ahead of him; she was the one who'd wanted the divorce. She was here now because he had to be part of a solution. Perhaps she'd already worked all of this out. He said, "Of course." He turned and moved in the direction of the kitchen. He reached for a plate from the cupboard. He used a serving spoon to work the contents from the shell onto the plate. He carried a bottle of wine and the plate out to the dining table. He went back to the kitchen to get two glasses and two forks. When he returned, he said, "Carpaccio's."

"How nice."

He could've been perfectly honest, told her he'd brought it home before she called. The food was here now, that was equally as true. He sat down first, reached for the wine bottle, poured a glass and guided it across the table. "Why's he calling you about this?" he said.

"I was his live-in stepmother there for a little while," Kelly said. Then, she decided to sit. "Why wouldn't he call me? His own mother is a troglodyte. He certainly doesn't want to face you, not here, anyway."

"Michael is twenty-eight years old..."

"He had a plan that he wanted to run by me. The plan, I thought, was not a good one. He simply wanted my opinion and he asked me to keep it a secret."

Her expression seemed matter-of-fact. He said, "How's teaching? How's your work?"

"Glad to have it," she said. "You?"

"We're bidding on a couple of projects downtown. We get one, we'll be all right for a year or two. What about your guy, mister what's-his-whatever?"

"What's-his-whatever is up in Boca for the weekend. Seeing to his parents. They can't sleep. I don't know what he thinks he can do about it. He's a terrible sleeper himself." She scratched at her cheek. "Look, Michael wanted to surprise you by showing up at the eight-thirty mass at Saint X tomorrow. He wanted to stand there in church next to you and then he wanted to go out for coffee afterward." Frank kept blinking. "He was going to tell you about the bookmaker then."

"Wrong," Frank said. "His plan was to get you to talk to me for him."

"He has his problems, but he's not stupid."

"What does the church have to do with any of this?"

Kelly's fingers touched at the neck of the wine glass. "I think that he thought it would be respectful. It's like he felt that if he put in a little time with you, then asking for so much money wouldn't seem so…reptile-like?"

"A reptile lives more honestly than that. He is a little hypocrite. I'm not giving him a dime. Let the bookmakers hang him up by his feet." She glared at him then. "What'd you tell him, Kelly?"

"I said it was a bad idea to approach you in that way."

"That kid has no spine."

"That's enough, Frank."

"We tried to raise him right."

"Easy," she said. "I know we did."

"Dammit, goddamnit." He put his index finger to his lips. "I'm sorry. I know you're trying to help. But I don't want to do this, Kelly." When he looked at her again, she swallowed, didn't speak. She hadn't touched her wine. He picked up his fork, took a bite of fish, then another. He said, "He made all those speeches when he was growing up about how lousy it was we made him go to church. Of course, he was very young. I felt that way myself when I was his age. When you're through making speeches, that's when it becomes hard. Have some." She didn't respond. "I don't go every Sunday, anyway," he said.

"No?"

"If I'm not in the mood to listen. Sometimes when I'm there, I kneel and stand and sit with the others. But the mass is the last thing on my mind…nothing's happening there…though I'll tell you, right before last Christmas, the priest, Father Hernandez, was giving a sermon, he was just going along about John the Baptist or something and then he kind of lost track…he started to talk about how people weren't dressing up for church anymore, I guess he was looking out at all these open-collar shirts and cargo shorts…he said, 'This isn't some vacation, this is a place of worship!' The silence that followed was ominous. The mass is very structured, but this time I had the feeling that no one knew what would happen next. He finally said, 'For heaven's sake, let us pray…'

"I always dress appropriately. But I think we all felt accused of something. People complained to the diocese, of course. It's unnerving to see something bothering a priest. That doesn't happen just because half the congregation is wearing sandals. The father took a leave after that. Hasn't returned as yet. I think that an intelligent priest must have such a complicated relationship with God…anyway, it was the most interesting thing that's happened in mass for a while now." He decided to lean back in his chair.

She said, "Waste of time."

He regarded her in a patient way. "Well, you've always been up front about that."

"I'm past my speeches, don't worry. Honestly, I'd do anything to feel differently," she said. "But I don't."

"Have some fish, that's easy enough." He edged the plate in her direction. She shook her head, picked up a fork.

"Michael just sees you as someone who is positive about all that he knows," she said. She began to eat.

"He wants to look at everything like a child, that's why. He might be running a con on us, he might only need five thousand. He'll take the rest to Gulfstream Park. It's possible."

"He sounds scared to me."

Frank decided to let her eat. She had a sip of wine. His hands were folded across his belt, and when he looked down at them he felt his age. Michael might've imagined that at mass was where he'd find his father in a most peaceful state of mind. "How'd you picture me reacting if he appeared at church tomorrow?" he said.

In a moment, she said, "It would frustrate you. His plan angered me some, too. I told him that when he reaches a certain age, he'll understand some things aren't what they once seemed."

"I keep trying to work it out. You could always tell."

"I know you want to know the truth about something," she said. "And that it conflicts with how you want things to be."

"The more I go, the more I doubt. I don't believe. There, I...but I keep going. It's not a tranquil place for me now." He drew in a breath, felt his shoulders relax. "You seem melancholy," he said. "Are you in love?" She didn't answer. He knew he sounded too serious. "I'll give you something for Michael. Of course, you know I will." Frank imagined Michael standing alone in a pew at St. X. He thought of how his son might look in middle age. Conflict-wise, he has a lot coming to him, Frank thought. He almost said it aloud.

She said, "What's his...Bruce...is worried about all of this not sleeping business. There is nothing I can do. I do love him, he's very gentle. But he is tentative, I wish he'd take charge of more things. After I talked to Michael, I started to think of my own parents. I was thinking about how they looked when they slept. I remembered one time on a visit to Atlanta when I went upstairs to see my father to tell him I needed to catch my plane...he was sleeping on his side, he was just wearing shorts and a t-shirt. His mouth was open, like he was in the midst of a long scream. He already looked...anyway, this afternoon I decided to get away from Miami Lakes for a little while. I wanted to see you in person...do you understand?"

"Yes," Frank said, in a deliberate way. "I'll sing and dance for you." This was better.

"Look, when do you think I ought to talk to Michael again?"

Again, Frank thought of Michael standing in a pew at church. He thought of the mammoth ceilings, the stained glass bright in the morning sunlight. "Call him after dinner. Tell him he doesn't have to bother with his plan for tomorrow. Let's give him half of what he says he needs. If he owes what he says he owes, he'll need to work out the rest. Half is what he is going to get. All right?"

"Half."

"He's lucky to get that." Frank wanted to say more. Instead, he took a sip from his wine glass. In a quiet way, he said, "He needs to come here to see me for anything else. He needs to..."

"Face the music?"

"Well," he said. "If that's what you want to call it."

* * *

When Kelly phoned Michael, she was in the guest room with the door closed. Frank opened the blinds in the sunken area of the living room; he liked to see how the sky looked at night. There were always the headlights of the cars moving along the beach highway. When the three of them lived here, there'd been too much drama. He couldn't recall what they each wanted then. He wasn't nostalgic for any of that now. He went to his bedroom and made out a check to "Cash" for $5,000.00, stuck it in the blue purse Kelly had left on the dining table. In the sunken part of the living room, he found a ballgame on TV.

Kelly emerged from the guest room, walked across the carpet and stopped a few feet from where he sat. She said, "I said I was here and you and I are working it out. I told him that he needed to start behaving like we weren't here to save him. Of course, he didn't like the sound of that." She spoke in a measured way. "He asked if we were sick. I said, 'Of course not, Michael. Good lord.'" The color in her face was high.

He nodded. Right then it seemed as if he had always missed her. But this wasn't the time to say that. "Here, sit down and let's talk. I'll turn off the game." She remained on her feet.

Kelly said, "You going to marry this...pilot?"

"No," he said. "She's here and then she isn't. I like her. But I am not marrying anyone else. Are you?"

"Who knows." She stood with her hands behind her back.

He reached for the remote, switched off the game. He said, "Would you like to stay tonight?"

"Would you like me to?"

He didn't answer.

She said, "Suppose your girlfriend wants to surprise you? She's already turned the plane around?"

"She loves Berlin," he said. "Anyway, I don't ask who she has a drink with while she's in another country. She tells me what she wants. Suppose Bruce wanted to surprise you? Maybe he's in back Miami Lakes right now, waiting."

Neither of them spoke.

"We can sit up and talk," he said.

She blinked. "Don't get old on me, Frank."

He nodded. He drew in a breath. "Was Michael upset?"

"Yes, he was."

We probably can't protect him from what he's really afraid of. He thought about saying this. "I'll be in," he said. She turned at that. Then the door to the bedroom door was closing behind her. He felt nervous but he understood it would be easy to make love to Kelly. That had never been their problem. Frank wanted to give her a minute, so he turned on the TV, muted the sound. The Marlins were playing against the Mets and losing 10-1. The stands were nearly empty. Frank thought of the first time he'd met Charlotte, in the Sky Club Lounge, and how she looked in her uniform. A decade younger than him; shapely, blond. She seemed to like living with him in her on and off way and he supposed their relationship might last longer because of this. When she arrived back here, he always wanted to hear about her travels. She'd spent a night in Vegas playing blackjack at Steve Winn's hotel. In Paris, she'd sat on a bench in the Tuileries Garden and watched a gaggle of young art students, each standing in front of their own easel. Someone there had a boombox that played music by the late, great Lou Reed.

He walked to the front door, made sure it was locked. Outside the bedroom door, he took off his shoes. When he opened the door, the light was on. Kelly was nude, her legs crossed at the ankles. She had a book but was holding it upside down. Something on Frank Lloyd Wright. She said, "I feel like being married to you for a few hours. That OK?"

He had his hands in his pockets and he shrugged. "Wonderful," he said.

"I'm going to turn off the light now."

They made love and as they did, she wrapped her arm around the back of his neck, pulled him close. She whispered to him but it was like he couldn't understand anything, and as he was climaxing she said, "Yeah, ride it out, all the way!" Then she let go of him.

Later, as he started to drift away to sleep, Frank listened for the sound of cars buzzing up and down the beach highway. He couldn't help but think of when Kelly was living here and how unhappy they'd been in those final months. Kelly was better off now; he couldn't tell about himself. Probably not. Almost certainly not. He supposed she was already asleep. He imagined what Charlotte might do when the sun came up in Berlin. It wouldn't be long now. She was alert about world times, always called when he was likely to be awake.

He fell asleep and the next thing he knew, the light on his side of the bed was on. Kelly had on the clothes she'd worn here; she sat on the edge of the bed, right at his hip. "What time is it?" he said. "Is it morning?"

"Almost," she said. "I want to get going. Going to go back home and change."

Frank wanted to make an offer. *Charlotte has clothes.* Right away, he imagined Kelly in a pilot's uniform. He reached for her hand and he wiggled it. "Thanks for thinking a lot of this through," he said. She seemed surprised at this and he let go.

She studied his face. "I liked some of it, too, you know," she said. "We'll all be alone one day."

"So it seems."

She said, "I have to meet Michael for coffee in a little while.

Then Bruce will be home."

"How much does Bruce know about Michael?"

"He'll know everything when he gets home."

"Not about this, though."

She tilted her head to one side. "Will Charlotte?"

He said, "Don't tell Michael…everything."

"I haven't."

"Did you get any rest? I'll make you something to eat."

"What are you going to do today, Frank?"

"Just sit here. Till I think of something else."

"You will. I gotta go. Bye."

"Bye."

He listened to her steps move across the living room carpet; the front door opened and closed. He imagined Kelly meeting with Michael at a coffee shop, her holding out the check, the two of them having another heart to heart. She might say to him, *One day, Michael…one day.* The news might not seem as hard coming from her.

It was Sunday morning and Frank didn't want to be alone. He decided to call Charlotte, see what she was up to. At this time of day, she might be surprised to hear from him. Where she was it would already be Sunday afternoon. She'd say, You getting ready for mass? It's so gorgeous here. Don't tell me you miss me already. The sound of her voice would thrill him.

Wake

At dawn on a Saturday morning, Toby steps outside in a sweat suit and sneakers and he spots a downstairs neighbor, Kate, who stands on a section of grass in their building's courtyard. She flings out her arm, tosses a handful of dust into the air. It's as if she is casting a spell; the mist disintegrates as it floats in Toby's direction. She turns a small box upside down, gives it a tap, and a tiny cloud rolls out. When she catches Toby in the corner of her eye, she eases the box behind her hip.

He's been waiting for a chance to talk to Kate and decides to move in her direction. The grass is neatly trimmed and the sky beyond her is wild with stripes of orange and saffron. She holds a hand to the side of her face, makes a half-megaphone, and mouths a word: "Ashes."

Toby's outside because he wants to run in the city park, which is right across the street. The lawns there are shaggy. There's an egg-shaped lake he likes to do laps around. Near the park entrance, two men in windbreakers stand under the cover of the bus-stop shelter, this even though the weather seems fine. One passes a cigarette to the other. Toby halts a couple of steps from Kate. She wears a long-sleeve gray t-shirt, yoga pants, Crocs. She's mid-twenties, a couple of years younger than him, has shoulder-length, dishwater-blond hair and piercing blue eyes. She touches the cuff of her t-shirt to the tip of her nose. Then she gestures to the courtyard lawn with an open palm. "This is my cat."

"You had a cat?"

"Him. Degas."

"Wow," Toby says, in a faint way. "The painter?"

"Like the painter. An orange tabby," she says. "I had him for only a few months. He got cancer. Died three weeks ago. I'm just now..." She turns the box upside down and taps the bottom. The residue drifts, then disappears. "There's just a vortex of ashes in here."

She produces a lid and secures it atop the box. She says, "Look at this thing. When I complained about the price, the crematory lady told me I could use it as a flower vase. I think that's a stretch." The box is made of tin, has a blue-and-green checkerboard pattern. She's holding this out to Toby. He accepts it and then she pushes loose strands of hair behind her ear. "I don't feel like being inside my apartment right now," she says.

He says, "Buy you a coffee?"

They watch one another for longer than a second. "Okay," she says. "All right."

Last fall, Toby's wife was in Montgomery, Alabama, on a sales training trip. The night before she was to return, he sat up alone in their apartment, drinking. At some point, he walked down a flight of stairs and knocked on the door of Kate's apartment. What he knew about her primarily was that she drove a Kia and at the HOA meetings was not afraid to complain about the rules. Toby had no idea what he was going to say. They were neighbors who lived on different floors and their relationship consisted of have-a-good-ones, see-you-laters. After he knocked, he heard footsteps inside. The door had a peephole. She kept the door closed, said, You okay out there? What is it?

He stood in a daze, couldn't think of anything. His tongue had just disappeared.

The door opened. She said, What's wrong?

He said, I'm free right now.

Jesus Christ. Please, go back to your apartment, go to bed.

He returned to his own apartment, drank himself to sleep. In the morning, Toby wondered about damage control. Kate probably thought, *Bland on the outside, awful on the inside. What a prince.*

Toby imagines that he looks like a man who is in need of something. And he almost always feels this way. His wife, who seems to understand many things, recently said to him, *I'll give you anything you ask for. You just need to say what it is.* Toby understands that she wants him to have what it is he thinks he wants so they can get on to the next thing, whatever that happens to be. The morning after he knocked on Kate's door, he had the urge to walk back down there again, say he was sorry. He thought better of it. What could he say? *I was polluted? Whenever I have a few 7 & 7s, I turn into Mr. Risk and Adventure?*

Kate and Toby walk up the street for the grill on 10th and Juniper. He carries the tin for her and he thinks of what he will say when his wife asks about his run. She probably imagines that he thinks about Kate and not just Kate. But this is not a source of contention between them. His wife's best friends are two pretty buff guys, Mack and Nat Powlight. They're brothers and one of them is gay, though Toby can never remember which one. He imagines that she thinks of them in non-platonic ways. She told Toby that one of them once tried to kiss her and she let him, just for a second. Sometimes, Toby tries to picture what she imagines if she could be with them. He thinks of Cleopatra.

The tin feels like a strange thing, though perhaps this is only because he knows what was just inside it. He says, "I've read about gamblers who asked for their ashes to be tossed onto racetracks."

"Yeah?" Kate says.

"I haven't made any plans about my own as yet."

"Maybe someone else has." She offers a little laugh, which he is glad for. Then she sniffles and says, "I was going to spread Degas in the park, but then I read they can actually arrest people for that. I thought, with my luck. All our mighty HOA can do is slap you with a fine."

He thinks about the courtyard lawn and how well manicured it is. The people who live in the building are educated; they have careers, work to do. There is one child among them. A Canadian couple on the first floor has a small, black-haired boy. Everyone is wild about him and they are equally wild about the fact that he is the Canadian couple's to raise. Toby and his wife have been married for eight years already. They bought a goldfish a couple of years ago and it was a lovely thing, swimming in its glass bowl. Following work, they'd pull chairs around the bowl and watch the fish while the late-afternoon sun streamed in through the windows. They talked about its color and how it might perceive things. How truly peculiar they appeared to it. Of course, they also got to chatting about their jobs, the bills that awaited them.

He and Kate step into the cafe together. They are shown to a table for two at a ceiling-to-floor green-tinted window that looks out on the street. They each ask for a coffee, then Kate heads for the restrooms. Toby can't decide what to do with the tin, so he balances it atop his knee. The sky is cloudy now and the light it gives off is grayish-green.

When Kate is sitting across from him, Toby says, "So, Degas. That's a great name."

Her face is pinkish, scrubbed. "I adopted the cat from a rescue place about six months ago. He used to climb around and take dumps on my magazines. Once I came home and found he'd crapped on a *Time* with Mitch McConnell on the cover. That's how he got his name."

Toby says, "Now that I know that, I feel sad he's gone…I didn't even know him."

She sniffs. "How's your wife? Her name's Jennifer, right?"

"Jennifer," he says, with a nod. "She's into selling at the moment. She's good at it, especially out in the 'burbs. She knows that buying stuff makes people feel like they still have a little power. She has an informed view, I guess."

"She from another country?"

"Knoxville, Tennessee."

In a moment, Kate says, "She's pretty."

Toby cannot decide what, if anything, Kate is trying to tell him. He concludes that she is merely stating a fact. He brings the tin to the table, catches a glimpse of a gold label stuck on the bottom. Paws, Whiskers and Wags, LLC. A waitress brings over two mugs of coffee and he sets the tin by his silverware. The waitress is younger than Kate, has her hair pulled back. She points to the tin with her pencil. "Is that what I think it is? A jack-in-the-box?"

Kate gives a patient smile and Toby twirls his index finger near the side, says, "Those have a little crank in the back. The old-fashioned kind. Needs to be wound up."

"Oh, yeah."

Toby nods in a solemn way at the tin. "Urn," he says.

Kate says, "He presents me with ashes, can you believe that?"

The waitress says, "That shouldn't be on your table, guys."

"We're having a wake," Kate says.

The waitress seems indecisive. It held ashes, Toby is ready to offer, if she wants to get technical about it. "Anything else?" the waitress says. Kate shakes her head, then Toby does the same. The waitress walks off.

Toby realizes that Kate is giving him a chance. He bows his head. "I am sorry about that, that one time."

Her eyes have teared up. "My cat never did anything to anyone."

She turns her profile to Toby then, watches what's happening outside. He sees himself at Kate's door. Then he pictures the two men in windbreakers standing at the bus stop. The bus stop is right across the street, he thinks. He feels like saying more about that night. This seems important. *I wanted to see you.* But he can't really explain it other than that. He says, "I guess I wanted to see what it would be like if we were doing something other than saying hello and goodbye to one another."

"Well, this is it." She seems to be less emotional. "Forget

that already," she says. "Jesus Christ. I'm not mad. I understand. When I heard the knock, my heart did a little flip. You just weren't who I was expecting."

"Degas, he painted ballet dancers. He did horse races, too, I think."

Kate, who seems lost in her own thoughts now, simply nods again. He tries to think of something amusing to say about McConnell.

The waitress returns, eyes the tin. She tears off the check, sets it on their table. Overall, she seems uncertain as to what they're up to. After she's left, Toby leans forward and says, "I don't have any money."

"Me, neither." Kate offers a faint, helpless smile.

"Dine and dash?"

Kate tilts her head to one side. "Come on, you're almost a decent guy again."

"Sure," he says.

"Sit here with me for another minute. So, what would you have said if I had opened the door for you?"

He says, "I probably would've talked about my job. How my boss is busting my ass."

"That would've been keen."

"I'm a catch," he says.

"Look...are you going to say anything about the ashes? I know the HOA is just trying to keep things nice. He was just a little cat, you know? I want to know he's around."

"I didn't see a thing."

"We just ran into each other."

"That's it. Let me get this." When he stands, he places his hand atop the tin. He feels like he should add something about the cat. "Tell her I'll be right back."

Kate blinks, says, "Yeah, I might go in another minute or two. I usually don't like to stay too long at these things."

Toby leaves the table, the restaurant, strolls down the street, lets himself into their building, walks up the three flights to his apartment. He hesitates in front of his own door, even though he has the key in his hand. Jennifer didn't sleep well last night, and he opens the door as quietly as possible. Toby is surprised to see her sitting up on the living-room couch, her hair in a tangle. She's in a bright green robe they pilfered last spring from their New Orleans hotel room. They thought they'd gotten away with it, but when they received their next credit card bill they'd been charged for the robe—a completely unreasonable price. She hasn't been awake for long, that's obvious enough. Toby's wallet is in the pocket of his blazer, which is hanging on a coat rack not far from the doorway. "Hey," he says. He closes the door behind him and stands there with his back against it. "What's happening?"

She places the butt of her palm up to her right eye, rubs it, then drops her hand down to her side. "How was the gallop?"

"Didn't do that. When I stepped outside, Kate from downstairs was tossing the ashes of her cat Degas in the courtyard. She asked me to take her out for coffee afterward. But then neither of us brought any money." He walks over to the couch and sits by her.

"Good old Kate," Jennifer says. Her tone seems knowledgeable. He has a sinking feeling that Kate has told Jennifer about the late-night visit and that Jennifer simply might've asked for Kate to cut him some slack. *He's used to having me around,* Jennifer might've said. She's speaking, says, "She told me her cat died. She showed me photos of when she first adopted it."

Toby finds himself nodding. He says, "Remember that goldfish we had? Blue?"

"Old Blue," she says with a somewhat groggy voice. "He was grand."

"What happened?"

"Well, he died."

"No, why didn't we get another?"

"We wanted to go through a period of reassessment," she says. "Of his overall significance."

He whisks his hand across his chest twice and then he says, "Did he have a little man in there with him? A guy in one of those old-time diver helmets at the bottom of the bowl?" He raises his hands, holds them apart. "Big iron helmet."

"I don't remember."

"Did the apartment feel empty without Blue?"

Jennifer's knees are crossed under the robe. "It felt like less," she says. "There is a difference."

"I didn't want to replace him, then have to replace the replacement. I was worried that our stuff would just start to blur together." He waves his hand at nothing in particular. "So what if it does?"

Jennifer is profile to him. She looks tired, but she is smiling. "You're in a good mood," she says.

"I love you," he says. "And I think I'm ready for a new goldfish. If you want. You pick out the stuff. The bowl and the stuff for the bottom of it."

"I'm gonna sit here for a few minutes. I'm glad you love me, that's good."

"I'll bring you a coffee and then we'll take the train up to that place, you know, the one with the laughing dogs on the sign."

"We can get the basic gear," she says, watching him. "But I'd like a frog. I've read they're disappearing. I don't think we appreciate frogs enough. Do you?"

"I like frogs…I'd like to keep one, or maybe two if they prefer company."

"Garden variety frogs. Nothing multicolored or anything. Nothing poisonous."

"Agreed…"

"I'll give it some more thought. We'll just get ones that've been overlooked…boy, I could use that coffee."

He walks back up the street and supposes that on the train ride to the pet store, they can talk about what they'll do after they bring back the frogs and the aquarium. All of that can be situated in their apartment and there will still be a big part of the day left. They went to a botanical garden last summer; one of the buildings featured a simulated rainforest. There were bright-colored frogs that lived behind glass, in their own exhibits. They were quite beautiful—and lethal in some instances. He is good with the garden-frog idea, but he wants to get a big-enough aquarium. When he and Jennifer came home from work one afternoon and found Blue dead, they blamed themselves, agreed that a larger fishbowl would've helped.

As Toby nears the restaurant, he can see through the street-view window. The table where he and Kate had been sitting is vacant. He arrives inside, walks over to the table and waits. In a minute, the waitress appears. He picks out a $20 bill from his wallet, holds it over and says, "And two coffees to go. She take the...thing?" With the eraser of the pencil, the waitress points at the tabletop, which only holds a small wire rack for sugar packets.

She returns, holds forward two large cups of to-go coffee. Then, his change. She says, "They tell us not to let people just walk off. I almost asked her to leave that...box for collateral. The lady said you were good for it, the bill, didn't want to hear about our policy... Is that what it really was? Ashes? She told me I could take off the lid, but I said no thanks. I'd find out it was a joke, that guy inside would jump out at me. I told her she could go, I wouldn't say anything."

Toby says, "It was the ashes of a rescued cat. Here." She has given him the chance to say just enough. He tips her five dollars.

"All right," she says and then turns and heads for other tables. The restaurant has filled with customers. They seem to have just popped out of the walls. Toby walks down the street carrying a cup of coffee in each hand. He takes his time, enjoys the morning breeze. Up ahead, he notices that the stand where the two guys had been waiting is now empty. They must've caught their bus. He thinks of the ashes from the tin, the way they danced in the air. Degas was loved. He hopes the cat had felt that.

Sequence

C, D, and E were the children of A and B. A, their mother, raised them to be gentle and kind. Because B, their father, was demanding, controlling, and difficult to please, C, D, and E grew up to be tentative people who lacked confidence. C married F, D married G, E married H. In their marriages, C, D, and E were submissive partners.

B demanded the marriage of C to F. This was immediately after A informed B that C, a college senior at the time, had called home crying, saying she'd missed her period. F's family didn't protest; marrying into the well-to-do family of A and B would be a step up for their lot. And C could not bear the idea of disobeying B. F got a job as a salesman, started coming home drunk in the evenings.

D met G in college. They were attractive, popular students. As G came to know D's family, he saw how their worlds revolved around B. He felt that D would stay loyal to a strong, confident man like her father. A man who believed the world was there for the taking; the higher the risks, the greater the rewards. After they were married, G worked hard and made good money as a stockbroker. He knew the market, but outside of it he was prone to making poor investments. He bought land in Florida that wound up with a sinkhole the length of a football field. He spent money on racehorses. D had to go to B on multiple occasions to cover G's losses. B always helped. To D, he was the greatest.

E dropped out of college to elope with H, a waitress with a high school diploma. They each were eighteen years old. They crossed the state line and stood before a justice of the peace. They spent their first night as husband and wife in a motel. They talked about running away, where they could go, what types of work they could do. They stayed up most of that night talking. In the morning, they talked some more. They'd been in a rush to get married. They agreed they didn't have a clue as to what to do next. So they drove back home to tell their parents. E went to see his, H went to see hers.

When E gave A and B the news about his marriage, A wept. This wounded E, who'd more than anything wanted to send a message to B that he could manage his own life. B asked A to leave the room. When it was just the two of them, B said that starting on Monday, E would be working in the family business. Otherwise, B would write E out of his will.

E left his parents' house frustrated and confused. That night, E and H stayed at a Holiday Inn. H reported that her parents were taken aback, but they were all right with her marrying into a family like E's. They said they hoped E and H were in love. They offered to pay for the hotel for a few nights. When E told H of B's reaction, H said maybe they should feel lucky that B had offered E something. It would be way better than anything E could get on his own without a college degree. E was stunned by her sudden display of pragmatism. He wanted to make her happy. He was married now.

* * *

C and F wound up with three children: a son, I, and two daughters, J and K. I, J, and K grew up in a household where the parents avoided confrontation. I suffered from depression and turned to alcohol early in life. J, who was named after A, committed suicide at the age of twenty-one. K eventually moved away. She was more attracted to women; it was a secret in the town and then it wasn't. C and F explained to their friends that K sought greater opportunities in the city.

D and G had two sons, L and M. G wanted them each to be

strong and independent and also to do exactly as he wished. Before each son left for college, G had a serious talk with him about dating and getting involved with someone who didn't share the family's interests. Couples with similar backgrounds were the ones that stayed together. G cited the quickie marriages of C to F and E to H. Me and your mother got to know one another, G said. Our parents approved, that was the important thing.

L, knowing it was impossible to please G, tried anyway. He married N, whose family owned a chain of successful dry-cleaning establishments across the Midwest. M, who came to understand there was no satisfying people who wanted everything, decided to ignore G's wishes completely. He fell in love with O, whose parents were teachers in the public high school system. M and O both turned out to be speech therapists.

E and H were, at first, tepid on the idea of raising a family. When they were twenty-five, they agreed to have a child, which turned out to be a daughter, P. Five years later, they decided to have another child; this was a boy, Q. H talked E into naming Q for B, which H felt would help to mend fences between E and B. It did not. B doted on Q (more so than he had with P) and this made E resent B even more. The truth was that B could be kind and loving, but a condition seemed to come with it. Even if B were somehow trying to redeem himself, E knew B would never admit he'd been too hard on his own son. What E took from this was that some things broken could never be fixed. His hope was that Q didn't turn out like either of them.

Like K, P grew up feeling more attracted to women. This created friction in the household of E and H. H felt there would be talk in the town; she felt A and B would be upset when they found out. (In fact, H had been one of those who'd gossiped about K; she'd said, *Well, if her parents actually belonged together, those kids would've had a chance.*) E felt they should try to understand and be supportive of their daughter. Like K, P moved away.

For a time, Q could not figure out what to do with his life.

In college, he cut classes, drank constantly. He was found one morning passed out under a campus security car. H heard the story from someone in town who had a son at the same college. Unbeknownst to E, H drove to Q's school. She surprised him, told him they ought to take a ride. She said she was going to take him home, put him to work, but she only wanted to get his attention. She drove for a few miles, then pulled off on the side of the road. Don't wind up like your father, she told Q. Look at how unhappy he is. Do something with your life. Be like B, cut out your own path. H suggested Q study law. H said, In the end, lawyers wind up with everything they want. She turned the car around, took him back to campus. When H returned home that evening, she told E she'd gone to see Q, give him a little pep talk.

Years later, Q would spill the details of that discussion to his father. By this time, Q was working in the public defender's office in the same town where he'd gone to college. He'd married R, a smart, attractive woman he'd met while playing doubles. They'd had twin sons, S and T, and a daughter, U. About once a month, Q would make the drive over to see his parents. He'd visit H at the house and then head for the country club to have lunch with E. H liked it that E and Q had their father and son time. At lunch, the men would talk about baseball, film, politics. E liked to hear of Q's plans; he wondered if Q shouldn't declare his candidacy for a seat in the state house. They agreed that the country overall had entered a dark phase. When Q was younger, he'd kept saying how the president (W) had set the country back by decades; where it was now seemed closer to the edge of an abyss. They agreed on that, too.

Q said he had enough work to do keeping his clients out of the state prison. Wanting to change the subject, he told his father he'd by chance run into M the week before. They decided to go out for a drink. They swapped stories about their college days. M told Q about the talk G had given to him before he'd gone to college—about who to marry and so on. M and Q laughed, they agreed that their fathers, all fathers, were completely full of shit.

To E, Q said, And to my children, I'll be full of shit, too. He was telling the story about running into M to tease E, whom he actually adored. Q also understood that E tended to be hard on himself, and it was important to remind him that everyone was rotten. E said their early father-son talks must've seemed awful to Q. And this was when Q told him about the time H had driven to campus to see him.

After Q told the story, E said, Some pep talk. When your mother said I was unhappy, were you surprised? Q said, No. E said, Are you sorry you turned out to be a lawyer? Q said, Sometimes. At the end of the meal, as they always did, E and Q bickered over the check. When he got home that evening, E didn't say anything about his lunch with Q, nor the talk H had with Q all those years ago. What would Q have done if he hadn't turned out to be a lawyer? E liked to wonder about that. Of course, Q could do anything he wanted. He had confidence.

By this time, E was in charge of the day-to-day operation of the family company. He had a middling interest at best in his work; and with him at the helm, the company had gone into a predictable decline. E wanted to talk with B about just selling the whole thing. He was working himself up to this. And then, with no warning, A died of a massive brain hemorrhage. She'd been in the backyard of the home she and B had shared for four decades, working in her tomato garden. A neighbor found her. Not long after this, B died, too. He had cancer; three months after it was diagnosed, he lay in a hospital bed nearing the end of his life. He told his children that everything he had done in life, he'd done for them. E understood that this could not possibly be true, but he didn't argue. Of course he couldn't. His father needed to believe what he was saying was true, he needed that to hold on to.

After B passed, E, at times, would feel like someone falling through time and space. He felt released; it seemed as if his life were just beginning. He also felt abandoned, alone, rudderless.

He began to consider his own decline, his mortality. The company was sold. The dividends for C, D, and E and their spouses didn't make rich people out of any of them.

G viewed the disappointing returns as an opportunity; he still believed they all should be wealthy. He and D hosted a dinner party for C and F and E and H. At the dinner, G laid out his plan; he made a pitch about starting a syndicate that invested in thoroughbred stallions, said he'd already looked into hiring bloodstock agents. Shares were available at four hundred thousand dollars apiece. By his calculations, each share would quadruple in value in only two years' time.

E and H listened, but they didn't have to talk it over. They'd already made their own plans. They were selling their house, the home where they'd raised their children. With the company sold and E spending more time at home, it was time to acknowledge how empty that house felt. The townhouse they planned to move into was half the size and it looked over the fourteenth fairway at the country club. E could take up golf again. With the dividends of the sale of the company, E and H would set up trust funds for P and Q.

At the dinner, E said he'd give G's investment opportunity some thought. G and F teased E about being overly cautious. *Life is short, life is all about chances!* A few days later, E phoned G to say he was passing. G said F had talked it over with C and they'd decided to buy into the project. E wasn't surprised to hear this. F was a gullible sort and C never objected to much of anything—though this isn't what he said to G. E said he hoped they all made a fortune.

* * *

With time on his hands, E began to more intricately assess his life. In particular, he began to focus on the subject of happiness. He should be happy: his children were healthy, his wife was still with him, he had this townhouse along the fourteenth fairway. He told himself he was happy. Sometimes it almost felt as if he were. But when he wasn't thinking about it, he slipped back into his unhappy, discontented self. Had he ever been happy? He loved his mother, as a boy only her presence had comforted him. He'd never liked school, had always been a restless, inattentive student.

He would think of the pep talk H had with Q. H didn't want Q to turn out like his father. Q hadn't. He was educated, assertive, poised. The question was, why would H stay with such an unhappy, unfulfilled man as E? He was the man she knew, that was an obvious answer. And there were a lot of worse men out there. E felt that if they'd just run away together right at the start, they would've been forced to live on their wits, find out what they were made of. They wouldn't have all this time now to sit around trying to imagine what they'd missed out on. If they had run off, how would things have turned out? They wouldn't be here, not in a townhouse on a golf course. E had a sketchy work ethic; he had no real talent for anything. He might've held on to a factory job, if they were lucky. He'd grown up around too much money and with too much of a father. He could've overcome these things, but something in him had sensed it wasn't worth it to try. As time passed, life did not get any easier. That was true for everyone. Why make it more difficult than it had to be?

E wanted to talk with H about all of this. They'd been talking about it for decades, he guessed. But they'd two children to raise, and he'd had a business to learn. After Q was accepted into law school, H earned her realtor's license and gone to work for one of E's friends in the real estate business. She'd done that for a couple of years, lost interest. E invested in a Baskin-Robbins franchise, and H became the manager of that. Despite its good location, the business had gone under. E wanted to make her happy. Had she ever been happy with him? He thought of the day before they'd married, when they'd agreed to go against the odds, go against what people expected of them. She was happy then. That was the best day of their lives.

P, their daughter, *had* struck out on her own. She'd moved away, earned her degree, wound up working as a copy editor of textbooks. She met V, a high school principal, at a dinner party given by a mutual friend. P and V were placed next to one another at the dinner table. Within a few months, they were living together. Not long after P moved in with V, E and H made the half-day's drive to visit them. P had been a morose teen, a moody college student. Now, she appeared transformed. With V at her side, P's eyes were bright with life, everything amused her, she took in stride the snarky comments H couldn't help but make. E and H stayed at a hotel in town that night; they stayed up talking about P, how wonderfully things were turning out for her. E was elated; P had been true to herself, she'd made her own way. She'd found love. She puts her heart out there, E said. It seems to be that way, yes, H said.

* * *

After being together for a few years, P and V separated. P was devastated. She began to drink heavily. On one of their visits, she told her parents her life wasn't worth living. She said she wished she'd stayed in their hometown, that as depressed as she felt there, it wasn't close to the agony she felt now. She apologized to her parents for being such a burden; they'd driven all this way to see her. She said she wanted to be left alone.

During that drive back, E and H talked about P's situation. H said, Well, when someone puts themselves out there, they're bound to get hurt. The way she said it made E feel bad for all of them. She can stay with us for as long as she wants, E said. If that's what it comes down to. And I never want to hear another word about what people might say. H said, I know how brave she is. She said, You act like I don't know that. But I do.

After being apart for nearly a year, P and V reunited. As it turned out, they each had their own lengthy set of flaws. They had heated arguments. But being apart was too painful for them. That same year, P and V invited E and H to their home for Thanksgiving. On the morning they were to leave for the trip, H told E that she was feeling spacey, a bit out of it. He should go. If she started to feel better, she might take a drive later, join Q, R, S, T, and U at their house. If not, she'd stay home, watch the Thanksgiving Day Parade on TV. By himself, E headed out to see P and V. During the drive, E felt free. It felt as if he still had the chance for a life other than his own. He almost felt guilty.

P and V were vegans and they laughed at his attempts to enjoy the mock turkey they served. Then, P brought out a plate with turkey and dressing as his reward. E loved it. He had an amazing time, and during the meal, he said he envied them. Everyone should be in love like they were. It didn't come out the way he wanted; no one spoke for a moment after that. He moved on to another topic. This is a great Thanksgiving, E said. Thank you.

He spent the night in a hotel, and in the morning, P and V came over to see him off. On the drive back, E tried to imagine what would happen if he and H agreed it was time for a divorce. He thought of practical things, who'd get the house, how they'd split the money. He'd feel isolated, he was rather certain of that. But would it be a great departure from the way things were already? Was it too late for him to look for the kind of love P and V had?

Most of all, now that he was retired, he wanted to talk with H about a great many things. Of course, they had time for this. They had all their meals together. They went to the country club for drinks. Afterward, they returned to their townhouse, had another drink or two. They'd talk about the syndicate G had put together, how unluckily things had turned out there. All zeroes. They were glad they hadn't gone in, but they hoped that G would hit it big one of these days. E would bring up something from the past when he and H were just starting out. She'd seem to lose interest. She'd grown quieter over the years; he'd noticed this.

* * *

One January morning, E and H were having breakfast at their kitchen table. His seat faced the sliding glass doors to the patio; beyond the patio was the fourteenth fairway, which that morning was covered in frost. She'd made pancakes and bacon. E was in a pleasant-enough mood; the night before, he'd had a dream about the bar they used to go to right after they were married. As he ate, he tried to recall the details of the dream. H said something about X, the president; E only listened to a little of that. Years earlier, they'd watched *The Apprentice.* A show that had amused them both. Anymore, they watched TV for hours every day. Everything blended together; reality, entertainment, honesty, culture, profits. As far as he could tell, all but the profits for the top one percent were in steep decline. He asked her what she remembered about the bar. Instantly, the subject seemed to make her cross. She said she didn't remember anything.

She said, You only married me to get back at your goddamn father. So let's just drop it, okay? E didn't respond, it seemed as if he couldn't. He glanced in the direction of the window that looked out to the fairway. He decided not to defend himself. He hadn't done anything wrong. He'd only been talking about a dream. Following breakfast, he pulled on a coat and took a walk. When he returned, H was stretched out on the living room couch, watching a rerun of the 70s comedy *Rhoda*.

The next morning, E and H were having breakfast; cheese omelettes that had been turned to scrambled eggs with cheese during the making. After she served him, H said, Oh, I forgot something. She left the kitchen and he heard the front door close. The electric garage door opened; a car engine started. A moment later, he could see her Saab heading across the fairway. He watched as it crashed head-on into the trunk of a box elder tree. E ran outside. Neighbors appeared from their houses, gathered around the Saab. H was leaned over the steering wheel. When the paramedics arrived, she was awake, looking up into E's face. She mumbled words, none that he could understand.

At the hospital, E was informed that H had a knee contusion, a sprained wrist. H had grown increasingly confused and scared and she'd been sedated. From the hospital, E phoned P and Q. He told them the doctors had suggested CT and MRI scans. Each of his children asked if it was Alzheimer's. E said the doctors said they wouldn't know that, not immediately. When E got home that evening, he spoke with C and D on the phone. Everyone was worried. E said he was going back to the hospital in the morning. He'd keep them all in the loop.

In a few days, H was allowed to come home. The tests had ruled out a stroke, a brain lesion. She had prescriptions for Donepezil and Galantamine. It was recommended she start back with the routine of her life. H seemed content watching TV. E and H were visited by their children and their spouses. Friends came by, so did C and F, D and G. E encouraged all visitors to be themselves, be natural, be comfortable. If H didn't respond to a question or a comment, it was all right. Don't be persistent, E advised. Just move on.

Still, for much of the time, it was the two of them in the townhouse, by themselves. E would forever be hounded by the guilt he felt. Why did this have to happen to her? Why hadn't he seen it sooner? He was always so lost in his own nonsense, the despair he felt. To converse with H, he had to remind himself to stay in the present. How's the pot pie? How do you feel? Would you like to take a walk? He knew that she knew so much more than the answers to his trite questions. But it was all locked away. They watched the news and E would say, What do you think? and H would say, I don't know. Or she would just shake her head. Once, E said, I feel sorry for his children. H didn't say anything. He knew not to pursue it. To E, the children of X seemed shallow and helpless. But, of course, they didn't have much of a chance to be anything else. If H were lucid, she might say he was projecting. He could only imagine that discussion. *How much control did people have over their own lives? Was the trajectory of a person's life unstoppable? Could anyone ever shake free of their destiny?*

When the COVID-19 pandemic engulfed the country, E ordered a box of disposable face masks. He wore one every time he left the house. Many of his friends did not. Before H left the house, he would place a mask on her. When he brought a mask to her face, she'd brush his hand away. E would say, You have to wear this. I don't want you to get sick. She would relent. He had masks for anyone who wanted to pay them a visit.

On a Friday afternoon in the middle of May, P called from the road, said she was just a half-hour away. E said, Is everything okay? You're just half an hour away? P said, I need to see you. Everything's all right. It's fine. I'll be there soon. He supposed it had something to do with V; something had gone wrong, they'd split up again. When he got off the phone, he sat down on the couch next to H. E didn't want to appear worried. He said, Our daughter is on the way. Yes, H said. Our daughter.

When P arrived, she wore a face mask; she held an overnight bag at her side. Her eyes were shining, and he could see trouble in them. I just wanted to come home for a day, to see you all, she said.

Later that night, after H had gone to bed, E and P sat up at the kitchen table and talked. They pulled the chairs back from the table. P said, I want to talk to Mom, by myself. I want to tell her she was a good mother. Before it's too late. Her eyes were blue like his and they immediately turned watery. E cleared his throat. He said, I understand what you're saying. I'll take a walk in the morning. It's supposed to be nice. P said, It wasn't easy, growing up here. Now I'm with someone I love, but we're cooped up, working at home all the time. It's not easy. It's like love can't save us. Our lives suddenly seem tedious and unforgiving...it's almost impossible being with someone you love so much. Oh, man, I'm such a mess right now...I'll be okay, P said. But I've seen how other parents can be. V tells me stuff, from the high school. They're monsters out there. All you have to do now is turn on the news. E said, I know.

In the morning, after they finished breakfast, E took a walk. The sky was blue and he felt the sunlight on his balding head. He watched golf carts heading up the fourteenth fairway. Of course, the groundskeepers had covered those tire tracks from last fall. They'd put down sod; you couldn't tell anything at all now. E wore a face mask; he noticed none of the other golfers did, even those riding in carts together. They'd wave, he'd wave back. He'd played golf for years, back when he'd been learning about how to run the company. He'd treat a client to a round. He'd always hated all that bullshit, all the small talk, the back and forth it took in order to get someone to write the company a check. He'd think, *God forbid any of us ever run out of money.* At golf, he was pretty good, had a natural, easy swing. When they'd moved here, it was thought he'd play regularly. But he hadn't been interested.

When he returned to the townhouse, H and P were sitting together on the couch. P said to E, Did you walk the whole course? P placed both of her hands on her mother's hand. I gotta go, Mom. At the door, she said, Thanks, Pop. Despite the concerns of the surging pandemic, she hugged him.

The next day, E and H were having lunch together. Tuna salad sandwiches. The early afternoon sunlight beamed in from the glass doors that led to the patio. He said, You know something, you and I should have run away together, right at the start. He thought about adding, *We would've been happier. We would've been better off.* H was chewing a bite from her sandwich; she liked his tuna salad. She said, Mmm-hmm. Thoughts ran through his mind: *I guess it doesn't matter. We probably would've wound up on welfare.* He said, We'd still have gotten older, wouldn't we? He promised himself not to do this again, to say things that could make her feel worse. When he looked at her once more, he said, Can I get you anything else? Hmm-mm, she said. Good, she said. I know you like that lemon in there, he said.

A few mornings later, while she was walking to the bathroom, H slipped and fell to the floor. She cried out, made gasping sounds. E told her to lie still and he called for an ambulance. At the hospital, she was diagnosed with a broken hip. From the hospital, E called P and Q, then C and D. He said he wanted to talk with the doctors again; he'd have more information for everyone tomorrow.

H spent two weeks in the hospital. The doctors recommended she stay under constant medical supervision until she could move around without so much pain. They recommended a hospice with inpatient facilities, the best one in the state was in Shelbyville. E spent time on the Internet reading reviews of the hospices here in town; the reviews online backed up what the doctors had been telling him. Some town, E thought. My town. Perfectly kept golf course, terrible hospice care.

Once H had been transferred, E made the drive over to Shelbyville every morning to see her. Before entering the facility, he pulled on a face mask. At the hospice, Y, the kind and thoughtful supervising nurse, accompanied him to H's room. Y explained to E that H liked to wear the face masks the medical staff wore. Y would ask him to wait at the door and she would go in ahead of him. He could hear Y speaking gently to H. In her room, E and H wore their face masks and sat in the chairs on opposite sides of the bed. H could sit up without feeling pain as long as she kept her knees apart. They watched TV. He'd find reruns of shows from the 70s and 80s, which she had always preferred.

They watched reruns of *Rhoda*. Yes, she'd say when an episode came on. E tried to recall if he'd ever asked her why she liked Rhoda's character so much. He had, certainly he had. He couldn't remember her response. He tried to understand. Rhoda was a New Yorker, she wasn't afraid of what people thought of her. She had style.

They'd watch an episode, then another. Rhoda liked wearing bright, colorful scarves, he noticed that. Back at the townhouse, he went to fashion designer websites. He wound up ordering two dozen silk scarves for H. What would Rhoda do in the time of COVID-19? He also ordered two dozen bright-colored masks.

* * *

There were plans for H to come home. He wanted the townhouse to be as she knew it. He wanted it to have everything she needed. He didn't know what to do about her Saab. If he sold it, would she miss it? One evening in July, he went to the garage, pulled himself in behind the wheel. He noticed that the open stick of cherry-flavored lip balm had melted onto the coins in the cup holder. The Saab had been repaired after she'd crashed it, but it hadn't been driven. He hadn't taken it out; it was her car. When she was back home, would she wake up in the middle of the night wanting to take a drive? He could settle the issue by selling the car. But it was her car. One by one, he freed the stuck coins in the cup holder. They'd keep the car. He'd hide the keys.

In one corner of the garage, he noticed his bag of golf clubs. Before he knew it, he was carrying a five-iron out past the patio to the edge of the fourteenth fairway. It was twilight, the course was closed for the day. He dropped a few golf balls to the grass. The green couldn't have been a hundred yards away, and he stroked a ball and listened to see where it landed. A ball hitting the green—that was a distinct sound as he recalled. He didn't hear anything.

First thing in the morning, before the course opened, he went out to collect the balls he'd hit. One had made it to the edge of the green. The others were short. A couple had landed in the sand trap. He then returned to the townhouse and prepared for the drive to Shelbyville.

He began to do this each evening. At dusk, when the other golfers were gone, he'd carry his five-iron and a dozen golf balls to the same place at the edge of the fourteenth fairway. When he went to bed, he concentrated on how the club had felt when he swung it. He could tell when he'd hit a good shot. He was a member of the country club and the club had rules about homeowners just stepping out onto the course and playing whenever they wanted. But no one would say anything. The neighbors would probably defend him: *His wife might have Alzheimer's, don't you know that? Leave him alone, let him play. He's never bothered a soul. Always waiting for others to tell him what to do. Missed out on his own life. Let him hit a few more.*

One evening, he stepped out to the edge of the fairway. He noticed the purple sky, felt the breeze blowing in the direction of the green. He stroked one ball after another. On the second to last one, he knew he'd struck the ball well. Then, he thought he heard a *tink.* The sound of a ball that had dinged the pin. He stared in the direction of the green. He thought about walking in that direction. No, he'd preserve the mystery. He'd check in the morning. He went to sleep that night thinking about it.

In the morning, he discovered one ball not a foot from the hole. He supposed it hit the pin and then nearly dropped straight down. It wouldn't have counted as a hole in one—after all, he'd struck the ball from the fairway. He wasn't even supposed to be out there. From the green, he stared in the direction of where he'd stood the evening before, hitting his chip shots. Beyond that spot was their townhouse. He pictured himself standing at the edge of the fairway at twilight, a silhouette of a man. That was all. It was a pretty morning, warm already. The fairway was empty.

* * *

That morning, at the hospice, E and Y walked down the hallway, a few feet between them. At the doorway of H's room, Y said, Good morning, dear. H was already sitting up in one of the chairs, her eyes on the TV set. Y stepped in; she reached H, leaned down, and whispered something in her ear. Then Y motioned for E to come over.

Y said, H, this is your husband E. Yes, H said, nodding. She wore a medical mask and had a Persian blue scarf draped over her shoulders. Y had told E that H liked the scarves he'd brought, but not the colorful masks. H didn't seem unhappy here, though E still felt home might be better for her. They could try that again, when she was ready. At home, maybe she could tell something, feel something, about the lives they'd had. Y wished them a pleasant morning and left the room.

E took the chair on the opposite side of the bed. H was watching an episode of *Good Times*, which was a show they'd both enjoyed when they were much younger. They loved the characters James and Florida Evans, who, despite living in the Chicago projects, were a happy couple. E was feeling somewhat upbeat. He wanted to tell her about the chip shot he'd hit the night before. He wanted to tell her he'd been sneaking out to the fairway at twilight, going against the rules. He wanted to surprise her, make her laugh. He wanted her to know that he knew that, great shot or not, the joke was on him. The rebel. The outlaw. He could make fun of himself and it would always hurt a little, though in an unexpected way it would give him strength. Over time, he'd built up a little of that. He'd always tried, in his own way. At times, it felt like he couldn't have tried any harder. She was the one who knew that. That had been the blessing. She knew him. So did their wonderful children.

He knew better than to try and talk about things that needed context. He knew it was important to filter his statements. With her, he didn't want to be simply talking to himself. He had all the time in the world for that now.

The sound on the TV was low. Over the years, they'd developed a habit of making conversation during commercial breaks. This was before she became ill. They would chat about this and that and then one of them would say, *Okay, it's coming back on.*

The credits were rolling for *Good Times*; following this would be an episode of *M*A*S*H.* He glanced in her direction, noticed how her silver hair had grown longer, it reached her shoulders now, the fabric of the scarf. The color of her hair looked rather exquisite against the blue of the scarf. He considered how to phrase what he wanted to say. He wanted to say that he was nothing without her.

He said her name. She didn't turn in his direction and he didn't say it again.

About the Author

Andy Plattner's fiction has earned a Flannery O'Connor Award, a Henfield Prize, the Dzanc Mid-Career Novel Prize, the Dr Tony Ryan Award, gold medals in novel and novella writing from the Faulkner Society, a silver medal in literary fiction from the Independent Book Publishers' Awards, and the Ferrol Sams Award for Fiction. His other books include *Winter Money, A Marriage of Convenience, Offerings from a Rust Belt Jockey* and *Dixie Luck.*

His short stories have been published by *The Literary Review, The Southern Review, Fiction, Paris Review, Epoch, Northwest Review, Shenandoah, Mississippi Review, Yalobusha Review, Sewanee Review, Cottonwood, Whiskey Island Review, Chattahoochee Review, Folio, Tampa Review, New Letters* and *New World Writing.* He has taught fiction writing at Clayton State University, Emory University, Kennesaw State University, the University of Southern Mississippi and the University of Tampa.